Praise for *His Hundred Years*

"With its crisp detail and dappled mosaic narrative, *His Hundred Years* is a Jewish immigrant tale with a difference. The initial milieu is Sephardic, Turkish, Ladino, not European, and the protagonist, a buoyant and irrepressible salesman, is the furthest thing from Arthur Miller's defeated figure. This is a finely written novel."

— Morris Dickstein, author of *Gates of Eden* and *Dancing in the Dark*

"A graceful, witty, and bittersweet story. In recounting the adventures of her irresistible, funny, and indomitable polyglot hero, Shalach Manot both recreates the world of Turkish Jewry and makes an original and compelling contribution to American immigrant literature."

— Elisabeth Gitter, author of *The Imprisoned Guest*

"This fascinating book by gifted writer and storyteller Shalach Manot reflects on the life of an unusual Sephardic man, his childhood in Turkey, and later, his adaptation to life in America. We follow his adventures and come away with a deeper appreciation and understanding of the Sephardic immigrant experience during the 20th century."

— Rabbi Marc D. Angel, author of *The Crown of Solomon and Other Stories*

"A beautifully compelling family drama set in Turkey and New York. It is episodically told and the pieces fall elegantly into place to create a satisfying whole. This is a very Turkish novel, and calls to mind the work of Orhan Pamuk. It is that good!"

— Ari Goldman, author of *The Search for God at Harvard*

"Shalach Manot's tale is an extraordinary book of hours, sparklingly composed of twenty-eight jeweled miniatures, altogether painting a fine life of consequence and sweetness. The hundred-year-old man emits the light of a man who was born knowing the meaning of life and who proceeded to live it. A lovely, true novel."

— Rickie Solinger, author of *Reproductive Politics: What Everyone Needs to Know*

"The 'arsenic of frustration' and the rush of love cooked into the same meal—many small portions create a reading feast in this tale by Shalach Manot. *Nobody* and *somebody* can change places in a second or a hundred years. This story shares the pain of exclusion, reminding us that sometimes we may be the ones doing the excluding. If our survival depends on our ability to see the world from the perspective of 'the other,' the other gender, our partner, *His Hundred Years* is an exercise we desperately need and one that beautifully illuminates the life forces that shape us."

— Reiner Leist, author of *American Portraits* and *Another Country*

"An extraordinary story told in an unusual way. As in oral folktales, events described don't happen directly, but are transmitted to us through the mediation of a storyteller. But the stream of the narration is modern, non-linear. Combining the elements of the oral folktale and the modern novel, Shalach Manot offers us something truly innovative."

— Eliezer Papo, Director, The Sephardic Studies Research Institute, Ben-Gurion University of the Negev

"What a journey! *His Hundred Years* is rowdy and absorbing, modern and ancient, provocative and calming."

— Tovah Feldshuh, actor of screen and stage

"Welcome Judeo-Spanish-American literature rooted in Asia Minor."

— Richard Kostelanetz, artist/writer

"Idiosyncratic, memorable—a great pleasure!"

— Kelly Anderson, director of the documentary, *My Brooklyn*

HIS HUNDRED YEARS

A Tale

SHALACH MANOT

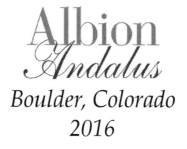

Boulder, Colorado
2016

"The old shall be renewed,
and the new shall be made holy."
— Rabbi Avraham Yitzhak Kook

"Canakkale, 1911," was originally published in issue 11 (Autumn 2011) of *Conversations,* the journal of the Institute for Jewish Ideas and Ideals, under the pen name Shalach Manot.

"The Kitchen in New Jersey, 1958," was originally published in issue LVIII.3 (Summer 2012) of *Midstream,* under the pen name Shalach Manot.

Albion-Andalus, Inc.
P. O. Box 19852
Boulder, CO 80308
www.albionandalus.com

Design and layout by Samantha Krezinski

Cover design by Daryl McCool

Cover art "Torah Ark Curtain" Istanbul (Turkey), c. 1735. The Jewish Museum, New York, The H. Ephraim and Mordecai Benguiat Family Collection. (www.thejewishmuseum.org)

ISBN-13: 978-0692633076 (Albion-Andalus Books)
ISBN-10: 0692633073

DEDICATION

To my readers —

Contents

Canakkale, 1911   1
Rodosto, 1915   5
Canal Street, 1936   9
Istanbul, 1916   15
Inecik, 1916   19
79th Street, 2000   23
Inecik, 1916 (II)   29
Inecik, 1916 (III)   35
2nd Avenue Shabbat, 2001   43
110th Street and 5th Avenue, 1920   47
Murray Hill, 1924   51
Murray Hill, 1925   57
Madison Square, 1926   61
The East Coast, 1927   65
Long Beach, 1973   69
Topkapi Restaurant, 1981   73
The Waldorf Astoria, 1964   83
The Telephone, 1965   91
Rodosto, 1915 (II)   99
30,000 Feet Above the Atlantic Ocean, 1972   103
Pine Street, 1988   123
Broadway in Brooklyn, 1982   129
Broadway in Manhattan, 1997   139
Boardwalk Along the Atlantic Ocean, 1958   145

******

Manhattan, Dinner at Eight, 1953   151
The Kitchen in New Jersey, 1958   163
Istanbul, Written in the Dark, 1971   175
The Atlantic Ocean, 2008   191

Glossary   195
Acknowledgments   199

Canakkale, 1911

"Shirts! Shirts!"

The boy was standing in front of the mosque just down the street from his family's house. Would you call it a street? It was dirt, it was never paved or stone, but as the men came out of the mosque, the boy sang out in a clear voice, "Buy a Shirt!"

He had said to his mother, "Zip, zip, you make them so fast, why not make them to sell? One seam here, one seam there, I'll sell them for you. I'll go in front of the mosque, and when the men come out I'll make some money, and bring it home to you."

It was the Ottoman Empire in 1911, in a port across from Europe—on the Asian side of the Strait of Dardanelles. They were living in a magnificent nowhere-land, with melons in the attic, beehives for honey on the windowsill, his grandfather's vineyards full of grapes, but with nothing much a man could do. Study the Torah—the Hebrew Bible—it was the most important thing. The men studied with the boy's father on Shabbat. But it was not enough. His father had the shop, with kerosene lamps and the dishes and glasses that came in huge wooden crates from Austria, but how many dishes could you sell in Canakkale? His father sat in the shop and read the newspaper. He knew how to read, so he relayed the news to everyone. What was the news? What did it have to do with them? Slowly, week by week the newspapers came from Istanbul and raised the same questions day after day. The lid was coming off, you could watch it jitter and settle and jitter again, or you could think about it.

The boy's mother was up at five every morning, sitting at the sewing machine. She sang as she worked, a steady breathing of thought and cloth strategy, her right hand on the wheel. She was like his father standing to pray, but she was seated with a firm hold on the earth, her foot on the treadle. Praying was breathing between here and God, and sewing was breathing between cloth and God, with a voice in Spanish words. The boy sat by her side, the cloth moved into creation while she sang. "*Ken me va kerer a mi, ken me va kerer a mi*? Who is going to love me? Knowing that I love you, my love for you is the death of me." But if cloth could become shirts, sung and sewn into creation, that you could wear on your back, then nowhere could become somewhere and a man could grow up through life like the turning of the events in the Joseph story, until the powerful man wept to see his brothers, and they all wept finally and knew even a boy thrown into a pit could grow up to be a vizier.

A boy could grow to be a man, might grow tall.

First the men took off their shoes, lining them up in pairs. Then with their clay *libriks* they poured water on their faces and their uplifted forearms, the sky overhead bright as a blue pillow of light, the breezes cool. Inside they prayed on the tiled floors. They did want the shirts, the men as they came out of the mosque. How could you say no, they were cheap.

Everyone needed a shirt at this price. Anyone would buy them, and it was the boy's idea. He had been proven right. Once as a boy you've been proven right, thinking for the family, you can keep going, jumping up in the favor of your mother's eyes, and your own eyes.

*

He was the oldest now. His oldest brother had been sent off to Jaffa to study the new science—agriculture. It was a scholarship from the Alliance Israelite Universelle. The very name of the school was like the bright wild shake of a tambourine to the mother and father, and to the five hundred Jewish families of the town. The boy himself went to the Alliance school in Canakkale. It was different from the ancient Talmud Torah with the children huddled around tables, taught by poor old shrunken men in raggedy beards. At the Alliance, Monsieur Toledano, the director who had studied in Paris, stood up tall and wore a top hat. The boy's mother had insisted the next brother go along with the eldest to Jaffa, although it tore her heart out to let the two of them go. But the Alliance was right that they had to save themselves from being ground into the earth and had to find the sea of emancipation. The sea was big, the world was wide, although the town was tiny, clustered, and safe like a breeze-blessed paradise at the center of the world. The town was at the Narrows of the Dardanelles, the same straits that were a birth canal for Europe, with the snow cold waters rushing down from the Black Sea through the Bosphorus through the Sea of Marmara to here where the ships of the world went by. His mother's rich brothers sometimes sat at the tables by the water (she didn't have the money or, with six children, the time to sit there), drinking tea, watching the ships of the world pass by with their colorful flags. You could see Europe right across the Straits, it was right there.

*

The boy knew the smell of kashkaval because when he worked at the grocery that year, the owner asked him to carry a whole half wheel of it across town. It was heavy for him, so to brace himself he carried it high on his chest, but his nose could not move away and the cheese was so pungent it stank. That smell he knew well (and eventually he would eat kashkaval years later). What the boy never knew was about Ovid's Leander, thousands of years before, swimming across the same straits in the terrible rushing current every night from Abydos on the Asian shore a short walk from Canakkale, to his goddess Hero across the water holding a light up in her tower. And he never knew about a limping rich English poet jokingly trying the same swim in the dark of night about a hundred years before the boy set up his gymnasium of branches and rope in a little garden. The boy did not know either about the nearby city of Troy, a half day's walk away, being attacked by the Achaeans across this same water—the Dardanelles, the Hellespont—and all the tales sung and then written down about those wars, jealousies, wrenching deaths and armor. What the boy knew was that among the Jews of Canakkale, the men sang the Hebrew prayers every day, praising the same *Ashem* the Jews had sung to after Ur, in Egypt, in the desert, in Jerusalem, on the Iberian Peninsula, and here where they were welcomed to settle and sent ships for, in the Ottoman Empire.

Rodosto, 1915

THE CAFÉS IN RODOSTO on the European shore of the Sea of Marmara were very smoky, especially in the wintertime. The men there smoked *nargiles*—waterpipes—and cigarettes all day. The boy could hardly see in front of him because of all the smoke coming from the men hunched and gathered at table after table. Maybe that was why the boy yelled his wares, although the other boys selling in the café made fun of him. But so what, who cares, he was a strong boy and did as he wished. After school each day he went from one café to the next and sold matchsticks and cigarette papers from a tray hung around his neck. Now he was truly the man of the family, not just as a joke to himself when in Canakkale he was seated next to his mother at the sewing machine and his two older brothers were gone. His father had grown a beard to make himself look old, then left Rodosto to hide in the big city of Istanbul. The father knew he could not even last a month in the Turkish army, and in the small city of Rodosto a man would stand out, and get picked up for the army. In addition, the father said he could hope to find work in Istanbul.

The men in the café complained that the boy was stealing matchsticks from the matchboxes. "Look, they're loose in here, some of the matchsticks are missing." At school, at the Talmud Torah—he would have liked the Alliance better where they slept that first night in Rodosto after Canakkale had been evacuated, but the Alliance already had too many children—the boy daydreamed fidgeting with the little layers of matchsticks, one on top of the other. They needed to be tight. In the Talmud Torah every day they sang the "*Hatikvah*." The boy walked his little brother to school. The boy shined the shoes of his little brother and two sisters and of the grandson of the people in whose hotel they had stayed at first. "Do you shine everyone's shoes?" the grandson asked, in surprise. "Why not?" There was food, and extra clothing, and the boy's mother quickly shortened the dress that was found for his sister, helped in the hotel washing dishes and serving the soldiers in the restaurant, and sewing and cooking to pay for their stay at the hotel. After the soldiers ate watermelon at the hotel's restaurant, the boy and his sisters and brothers would get the leftovers, juicy and bright.

The boy had no idea that, on the peninsula fifty miles south of where they were on the Sea of Marmara, hundreds of thousands of soldiers had landed, scrambling up cliffs or along ridges into machine gun fire and dying, or digging themselves into trenches, first in the glaring bright heat of summer, then in the cold, writing down their thoughts in journals over bully beef tins or praying heroically to Allah and eating their bread and olives. The boy had never heard of Australia or New Zealand, or Ireland or Scotland. He had never heard of Rupert Brooke or the crazed zeal of men for the romance of war. He knew, however, that the air was getting cold, and the men in the cafés smoked to hope and smoked

to forget and smoked to worry. If you packed in the
bottom layer of matchsticks very tight, then created
the second layer from two or three diagonal sticks,
a third layer on top could be packed in very tight so
the box looked full. It worked. Nobody said a thing.
He made four boxes out of three.

CANAL STREET, 1936

THE CANAL STREET STOREFRONT of Manhattan Novelty Corporation, wholesale importer-exporter, had the door propped open to keep the air moving. Of the two owners, one was crabby, short, with a nasty mouth and greedy pockets, the other was tall, a dreamer, a tailor's son stitching the responsible pleasures of wife and son in their Bronx Park East apartment to the job of running a wholesale business on Canal Street. The tall one always said half a loaf is better than no loaf at all and liked the occasional but steady flow of seekers and purveyors who came in the door in caps and fedoras, including buyers from Macy's and S. Klein, and men off the ships putting down leather goods samples on the glass display case to be fingered and smoothed over. The window held Hutch baseball gloves and bats, silver jewelry, Westclock timepieces, wallets, the traditional Canal Street cluttered display of untended miscellany.

The salesman who saw the open door had been working Canal Street and was trim, eager, white, in a three-piece suit despite the hot weather, and with deep brown eyes and a hat pushed back on his head. His people were called dark-complexioned in 1920, these stragglers from Dardanelles, carrying a mattress, a sewing machine, a tambourine, some old books, when the steamship arrived, and his mother's trachoma sent her back to Piraeus with his father.

But six months later the parents were allowed in and rejoined the four sons and two daughters, and the cousins and neighbors. That was the way of it, set back, and going forth, set back and going forth, set back and going forth, since Abraham left the City of Ur, and had to lie that his wife was his sister.

The salesman had married finally just two years before. Progress held steady, it didn't matter that it took until he was over thirty to marry; the depression made lots of things wait. She was smart, stylish, cooked the food he loved, and was only mildly terrifying. He thought he could handle her. He wooed her with French lessons. She hired a dressmaker to copy the wedding dress in Saks's window. They'd had a honeymoon—her idea! The salesman's posture was vigorous, his walking was brisk; if Canal Street were a hundred miles long it would have been easy, and he would only want more. Ten, twelve years of daily tenement stairs of selling had given him the vigor of an Olympic athlete, the men you saw in swimming costumes in the newsreels. Everything had made this breadwinner strong. Four, six apartments on a floor, five landings, speaking in four, six languages, knocking on every door, it was candy to him.

The tall owner of Manhattan Novelty was willing to be friendly back; he got it that everything was possibility. People often liked that notion on the salesman's face. The other owner disappeared, gave his back to the insurance salesman, annoyed that his partner even let the guy get to first base. What the hell was wrong with him? Was he going to give open session to every leech and parasite who walked in the door?

Yes, the tall owner said, he had a family, a two-year old son. They lived in the Bronx. The owner asked about the salesman's name—it's unusual—what kind of name is that? The salesman said it went back to ancient stories.

The salesman liked his work—in the depression, you could sell insurance just like you could sell baseball gloves. These were necessities, if anything was. Desperate for security, people would put down their twenty-five cents a week, be happy to see the handsome young man who came to your door every week, liked your children, always had something nice to say in your language, and interrupted the steady hours of drudgery in the cramped rooms with praise for the domestic arts, and bearing witness to a family's perseverance. In a tenement, just to be seen and recognized in a scrimping subsistence, to be seen with empathy for the desperate efforts to survive, was worth the twenty-five cents. The salesman had known about hunger and knew the determination to survive on nothing.

No bearing witness here at Manhattan Novelty. The tall prospect was like the salesman—a fellow husband, provider, someone who had found a way out ten years earlier from peddling cigars on the street. The business transaction did not take long. It was the beginning of a friendship. The salesman didn't just want to sell you something and disappear. He cared about you. He wanted to become your friend. His sincerity was a little crazy. It was a pleasure to take in everyone as a friend. He wanted everyone as a friend.

The salesman slipped in the name of his famous company slow but fast, with a smile. What the salesman knew about was family, that men had families their desires focused on, families that went back in time to parents and grandparents and forward to the future with wives and children. Working men had families they wanted to protect. That's why they worked. Insurance was a way of making all that work hold into an unknowable future.

"A two-year old boy—" the salesman said, "then you probably already have a good insurance policy. If you want, I can take a look at it, and give you an evaluation of it. You know that building on 23rd Street, the one with the big clock. That's the company I work for. The hands on the clock are so big, the minute hand is seventeen feet long. You're pretty tall, I think about six feet two inches (I bet your father wasn't so tall), and the minute hand is almost three times your height. You want to be sure you have a good policy, not just any policy."

The tall prospect was smiling. This salesman was adrenaline and charm, part business, part dream. It was a slow hot day anyway. The factories upstairs must be awful. Canal Street traffic rumbled by, and a truck raucously called attention to itself with a change of gears. The prospect turned the coin and asked about the salesman's family.

"My family came from Turkey, yours probably came from Russia," the salesman said. "I could speak to you in Spanish, Italian, Turkish, Greek, Armenian, or Hebrew. But I don't want to waste your time, you probably have life insurance already, and don't need to consider a policy from the biggest insurance company in America."

Again the smile. "I don't have a life insurance policy at all."

"That's why you're smiling. You're happy that I walked in here. This is a beginning, this is something you've wanted to take care of, and you've been so busy running this company, you just haven't gotten around to it. It looks like a pretty successful company. You sell so many different kinds of things here. It's pretty impressive, you get merchandise from many countries. You need to know how to evaluate things, and people. That's the important part, evaluating people. How did you get started in this business?"

The tall man could picture his partner smirking behind his back but here was someone to talk to who didn't smirk, probably didn't know how to smirk. Here was the poetry of salesmanship.

"I'll tell you what," the tall man said. "Tell me about the policy you want me to buy, then I'll think about it."

Istanbul, 1916

How would you go from Rodosto to Istanbul, at night, a boy with nothing? By ship of course, on the Sea of Marmara, due east. His mother gave him a warm coat, and into the lining she packed the bits of food she had collected for three days for the night's journey. It was a crazy plan, but maybe the boy could bring back his father. The boy liked to do what he wanted, so why thwart him when his fearlessness— and her older daughter's teaching herself to play the *chanun*, the zither—were all they had? The Turks had beaten the Europeans from Gallipoli, what a whipping. It went on for months too terrible to think about, with deaths on both sides that no one would dare to count, but now it was a time to take chances, because there was no food anymore, and the boy had to do something.

He planned it so well that in ten hours he was next to his father. He got on the pier and waited until a boat came in. He got in there. A lot of soldiers were lying down there. It must have been ten at night. He spoke to them in Turkish. He said, "I want to see my father, he's in the army in Istanbul and I have no ticket, can I hide with you?" The boy knew to say exactly the right thing. They took care of him as if he were their own, covering him with their blankets. No one could see him. Luckily there was a steam pipe that kept him warm.

It wasn't easy to get off the boat in Istanbul, but the soldiers told him what to do. They placed him at the exit. They yelled at him, "You can't come in here— get out." That really worked. He wasn't afraid. The strange thing was all the fears came afterwards. But he was out. He didn't have money, but he had an address. He started walking. Of course, Istanbul in the morning light was a big place. When you mail a letter, it goes directly, but walking it takes a long time. His hunger didn't bother him, he chewed on his determination, going forward, asking questions, a boy in a vast city he had never seen before. Carts rattled by on the narrow streets, the muezzins called out to the world. How could a place have such endless numbers of buildings, but he found his way. His father was glad to see him and wasn't glad to see him. His father was worried, how was the boy going to get back?

The father was a bookkeeper for some people in Istanbul. The boy embraced him and said, "Come home, mother wants you." But the man reasoned with his son, that was the kind of father he was. Only afterwards did the boy think about all the fears the father had. If they caught his father for the army, he was dead, worse than dead. So they had lunch, and walked around the city looking at rich merchants and long crowded streets. They learned that a ship was leaving for Rodosto at one in the morning. A lot of merchants were on the pier. The father said, "You'd better get on that boat now. You can't wait until an hour or two before it leaves. Go now." So he got something for the boy to eat and, in his short coat, the boy went on the ship as if he belonged there. It was during the day, and they didn't expect anyone at that time. He went all the way to the top between two smokestacks, one here and the other there. Nobody saw him or bothered him and he slept there; before he knew it, he heard the dooop, doop, the sound of a ship leaving the city. He was freezing. He ate the little bit he had to eat. The boat was going. The wind was blowing. He was freezing so he went closer to one of the smokestacks to get warm. When he got home his mother was so happy, she didn't know what to do for him. She gave him the only thing she had, *mushpulas*, little red pears the size of eggs. He told her his father was all right, and he repeated their conversations. She asked how his father looked. He said his father had a big beard and looked thin—like a skeleton. The boy felt big and strong. He had accomplished something.

But he could see that in Istanbul everyone except his father was making money. For most people in Istanbul there was a lot of money. Here in Rodosto there was none. Ideas swam in his head. He would do something.

INECIK, 1916

THEY HAD NO MONEY or food to eat or place to sleep,
but the boy and his mother opened a store in Inecik, a
four-hour walk into the countryside from Rodosto—
as if you had backed away for four hours from that
city on the Sea of Marmara dreaming of fields of
wheat. Would you call it a store? It was no store, and
in Inecik, there was no such thing as a store; it was
a hut at the edge of a big field, where the boy and
his mother slept on the dirt floor, and cooked over
a small fire when they got some food. It was empty,
and they needed to find a place to sleep because they
couldn't walk back to the city that day, their second
day in Inecik, even though the boy had bought a
pair of shoes from a man who had probably stolen
them from a dead soldier, shoes much too big for the
boy, and with nails in them holding the sole on; they
looked like they could hold the sole on for a hundred
years, for a hundred boys' lives; the big strong nails
could outlive a hundred wars. A farm-woman jutted
her head in the direction of the hut, as if to say no
one is sleeping there, go sleep there with your boy.
He was a boy, so she could acknowledge him in her
glance; in fact it was his boyhood that allowed him
to go with his mother to the farmhouses, and peddle
to the women and climb the tree when they got to
the first house to gorge himself on unripe pears that
he could not stop eating. But soon the hut was the

boy's dream come true, every peddler's dream; the hut had a roof but was open in front (a plaster wall gave them a room with a window in the back) and the buyers and country children looking for the new thing the way children always want the new thing, came to them instead of the other way around, to see what this was, to exchange thread, needles, and fabric for bread. The countryside was a paradise for bread; in Rodosto, the cupboard was bare. The British submarines in the Sea of Marmara had stopped the supply boats, had stopped everything, the overland mule trains were slow and the Ottoman heroic winning streak (the Turks had proved the straits could not be forced) had slipped out of sight as quietly as the British had slipped out of Gallipoli itself.

Four hours on a dirt road: the breezes in the wafting air were as light and empty as their stomachs. The blur of hills and fields and land in bright sunlight was as rich as hope could paint. The boy and his mother were partners. His mother put on a scarf and tied it under her chin. They had left the two sisters and the smallest boy in Rodosto in the care of the Armenian woman; the two travellers would bring back bread for all of them, because the countryside had it, the land had food, and who else had struggled forth from the coffee houses and bare streets of Rodosto undaunted to go find it?

In Rodosto the boy had watched the country people who, when they wanted needles, buttons, thread, and *yiminees*—headscarves—would come in with their camels to the market. They came to sell skins: horse skins and donkey skins to make shoes and saddles. The camels settled down on their knees in the streets, their mouths moving while the men sold the skins. The big mouths chomped droopingly as if the camels were lords looking over the city and couldn't care less. But the boy watched the men and their camels hungrily. When the Turks from the countryside stopped in the streets to pray, you didn't disturb them. The Turkish country people were a school for survival. They were not frightened or hungry. They were well fed and at ease, clustering in their robes and pants, squatting on the sidewalks to eat and confer. Their fields and chicken houses must be full enough. They were not like the rich merchants and hotelmen of Istanbul, but still you could smell in their complacency even their small storehouses of grain waiting for them at home.

The first night in Inecik, a woman said they could sleep on her cement porch. It was an elevated piece of cement floor sticking out from the house, and it wasn't as good as sleeping in the house, but not as bad as sleeping in the fields on the dirt. They were still part of the human family, peddlers, not interlopers or starving remnants of human life. They were recognizable in their role. Of course, the whole human family was forlorn and broken up with the vast war wracking the empire, the men mostly gone, the women working the land and keeping the farms going. The boy and his mother had no quilts to sleep on. They had only brought themselves and what they were selling. But with bread in their stomachs and lying down, they could stretch out their limbs and feel the ease of weariness and relief, splaying their hopeful thoughts open in the pitch black night into the wildness of sleep. The boy woke suddenly to the smell of animals in motion who were stalking and sniffing the cement floor and his body on it. His mother was awake next to him and signaled him as if by a silent infinitesimal thought to stay still as the animals brushed by. He could not see his mother's face in the dark, but he knew her calm dumb internal shouting down of fear in her mind. They froze; they became as still and dead to the world as the cement itself, with no laying out of breath, no human breath, as if they could suddenly stifle by sheer will the smell of themselves, human animals in fear, mother and son. Soon the *lobos*, two large wolves, moved along with their sniffing and seeking, and found something of more interest: the chickens in a pen where the dirt road and the dirt yard met, tasty and bloody and a good meal, full of squawking and feathers and fight. Now the wolves had fullness in their stomachs too, and could wander off to sleep.

79TH STREET, 2000

As HE WAS WHEELED down the wide tree-lined city sidewalk, the very old man sang the *"Marseillaise"* with the woman who was his grown daughter. Her hands on the two handles jutting out from the back of his chair, she pushed him along. It was unusual: a man in a wheelchair singing out loud in perfect French as he was wheeled down the street, but no harm done in creating a new curiosity on the streets of New York. Singing encouraged him to take deep breaths, lift his chest bone, and invigorate his whole thin frame; and *"Allons Enfants de la Patrie"* always reminded him that life was for pleasure and courage. As for her, it did the same. He had his cap on, and the suede jacket she had bought him years before, and a wool scarf another daughter had given him. He was dressed when his daughter came to pick him up at the nursing home. She had come across the park on her bicycle, locked it up to a street sign pole, and the effort spiked her energy, so once they were out in the air the *"Marseillaise"* came naturally to them both, and the few passersby looked up with interest and without taking offense. She said it was Saturday and she wanted to take him to the synagogue.

On other Saturdays, for instance in the summer, the synagogue was pretty empty, but it was fall now and would be different. The Caribbean-American guard appearing at the side door, his dark skin handsome against his sky blue uniform shirt, had pointed to the hallway at the back. In the summer they had followed around to a small intimate chapel where twenty-five people were led by a thoughtful volunteer and clustered on benches on two sides of a narrow aisle, then in the small entryway shared a challah afterwards by pulling it apart raucously so everyone had a piece. But today they went to the main sanctuary, which was packed for a double bar mitzvah, and the senior rabbi was in full flourish at the front, up on what would be called a stage if this were an auditorium, not a sanctuary. The well-dressed congregants and numerous guests (including, one might surmise, many or most who were entirely new to this synagogue, or perhaps any synagogue) were attentive, obedient, and well-groomed in their dresses and suits; in fact the rabbi even talked about the custom of standing in synagogue, a minor but significant exertion, which then everyone proceeded to do, because it turned out the synagogue was celebrating Simchat Torah that morning, with two *hakafot*—processions carrying the Torah scrolls around the synagogue—right then. The night before, the rabbi explained, they had done three, and he must have said something about when they would add the additional two, but in any event they added up to seven, as he briefly explained. The daughter was thinking about this rabbi's arithmetic for the holiday which did not begin in her synagogue (and presumably most synagogues) until the following night, and which would entail seven crowded processions sung with the verses of "*Mi Piel*" and six other celebratory songs both in the main sanctuary and the enthusiastic women's service. Her father listened and watched attentively but heard nothing about arithmetic. They were off in a little section all the way over on the right, perfect for wheelchairs, although they were the only one, the area which the guard had pointed out and which had allowed them a grand entrance rolling forth down the aisle in the packed synagogue when they arrived. When they reached the designated spot, they had properly positioned themselves there with good decorum.

The daughter had noticed an underdressed, overweight woman, perhaps also from the nursing home, in a thin housedress allowing rolls of flesh to pour out at the armpits; so the man in his wheelchair and his daughter were not the only self-invited guests. But the old man, not distracted by commentary which he couldn't hear very well anyway, was concentrating on one thing: the deep blue velvet-robed Torah, three feet tall, as it was lifted out of the ark. It was the same Torah he'd seen in every synagogue where he had ever been. As a boy in the synagogue, when everyone stood, he stood of course too; what else would you do in the synagogue but watch and listen transfixed and do what the others did as much as you knew, swept along with the intent of men doing what they knew best for millennia, and which told them who they were, and brought them together for their communal feelings, expressed through a ritual as familiar as eating.

When the old man managed to stand himself up in front of his chair, which took an intensely focused exertion of his two hands on the arms of the wheel chair, with his daughter helping him, his alarm went off. It was a thin high-pitched sound that careened eerily into the sanctuary with its own importance. People turned in surprise to look at them. The daughter had forgotten to disconnect it, but it meant nothing to him. The daughter fumbled at his shirt collar while helping him remain standing, and disconnected it now, as quickly as she could. He was focused on the Torah and the three or four men and women in their business clothes who were trailing behind the man who carried it in the silent synagogue, going across the front of the sanctuary, and down an aisle. It was coming near him now, and seated again in his chair, so that he could have a hand free, and feeling safely balanced in his chair, he reached out to touch it. His hand was right there, and he touched it. He breathed with pleasure and ease now, reconnected to his beginnings as if by a very much longer string than the alarm which he had sounded. But the relief brought tears. His dignity allowed itself this pleasure of welling emotion and relief from the uselessness he felt sitting in his wheel chair near the nursing station at the nursing home.

Well, he could still be useful by being cheerful and courtly, speaking in French to the Haitian nurses who laughed and eased into Creole themselves with him because it was like his French.

The very old man could in fact stand, and even walk around his floor in the nursing home with his rolling walker and an attendant next to him to support him if necessary, but the wheelchair was a necessity for any outing beyond his floor. Often, like the others, he would be seated in the wheelchair in the hall, with the alarm string tied to the neck of his shirt or sweater so that if he tried to stand on his own or leaned forward and started falling out, a nurse would hear the sound and run to prevent a fall. Sitting at the nursing station, with its ringing phones and the flurry of women in white hovering like birds, he always wanted to cry out, "I'm wasting my time!"

Touching the deep blue velvet-cloaked Torah in the packed synagogue was not wasting his time.

INECIK, 1916 (II)

How would you carry a large pot of honey a four-hour walk from Inecik to the city of Rodosto? In your arms, of course. Ox-carts and wagons passed him as his hands grew stiffer on his treasure. His legs were strong, carrying him forward across the long roll of the countryside, one foot in front of the other in his big shoes, but the worry that he would not be able to manage the task of carrying home the heavy pot of honey was long and monotonous. He sang songs he knew from his mother, like *"Elohenu Shebbah Shemayim,"* a counting song from *"Kualo es el uno, uno es el kreador"* (What is one, one is the Creator) to the eight days for the *brit milah*, the nine months of pregnancy and the ten *komandamientos* of the law, all the way to thirteen. The songs, the longer the better, carried him forward, like *"Ken Me Va Kerer a Mi,"* —who is going to love me—because it was an angry love song that his mother always sang laughingly proud that she had a good husband and was not the abandoned woman in the song. *"Ya Se Va Dormir"*— you're falling asleep now—was a lullaby he sang as a joke, because he was afraid if he stopped and rested, the honey would never make it home. Then came the special treats, the blessings from his father, *Sabri Maranan* (Attention, Gentlemen!), *Baruch Ata Adonai*, blessed art thou Lord our God—blessed was the woman who suddenly thought these poor people in the city are starving, let me give the boy a pot of honey to bring to his family in Rodosto; the "*Marseillaise*," the triumphant French anthem he'd learned at the Alliance in Canakkale; and the Greek song, "*Samiotisa*," that he heard that man singing in the fields, about the beautiful girl of Samos he had to leave behind. But when the singing was too much exertion, he just said the words in his mind. What was the drudgery of hills and land and the huge endless wild blue sky, plain hills and land and sky, unless the songs gave them meaning? Everyone in the house in Rodosto would see the honey and be shocked into joy. That was the song that his heart was singing. They would dip stale crusts of bread into the honey. The boy was their liberator from the terror of hunger.

Still, the idea only occurred to him when he was in the Rodosto market the next morning. He sold his *yiminees*—headscarves—quickly, buoyed by all the hard bread he had dipped finally into the honey that he had not tasted with his little finger until his arrival. His older sister's excitement, combined with finally enjoying the honey, gave him status in his own eyes, and that night he slept.

Two *yiminees* put coins in his pocket. He was standing looking around at the men selling their wares. The grey animal was standing there too. Big ears, big eyes, solid legs to stand on.

The boy had sold the brightly colored *yiminees* from his mother's cousin in ten minutes. It was fast, like eating candy. He could have sold a half dozen if he'd had them. The money was burning a hole in his pocket. He'd never bought anything except halvah and *simites*—sweet sesame pretzels—on the way to school, or his shoes. He knew nothing about animals, all he knew was songs, and to keep his wits about him. The donkey was looking at him. A donkey could carry. He walked over to a man standing nearby and in loud surprise heard himself say "*Ne kadar*"—how much?—at once brusque and timid because he knew once a salesman catches you in his net, you won't get out. It was like if a young man talked to a young woman it would be understood immediately that you intended to marry her. The salesman sprang to life, took hold of the boy's hand and brought him over to the man whose donkey it was. The man showed the boy the donkey's teeth. It was not easy opening the donkey's mouth. The man said it was very young, a baby. The salesman put the boy right there, and clasped the man's and the boy's hands together, and wouldn't let go. The salesman's two hands moved the buyer's and seller's hands up and down like a meter. Prices up and down made the hands go up and down, up and down, the salesman shaking the boy's guts with fear and pleasure until the deal was made, to exchange the money he had just made from selling two *yiminees* for the donkey.

The boy didn't get on the donkey. He didn't know how to get on it. He was afraid. He figured when he got to Inecik he had a lot of friends there who would help him. The seller told him certain expressions, but the boy was too excited to remember them. "Hit it if you want it to go," was all he remembered. The man gave him the bit to put in the donkey's mouth. It was early enough to go to Inecik the same day. He would surprise his mother in Inecik. He couldn't keep the animal in Rodosto because there was no yard or place to keep it. It was a donkey, it belonged in the country.

When he walked the donkey the three blocks from the market to the house of the Armenian family, near the neighbors who had also come from Canakkale and now lived across the street, it was the talk of the block. The neighborhood was moving up, as if he'd bought a fancy car. All the kids surrounded him, wanting to ride on the donkey. And to think he had bought it on his own initiative—without consulting anyone about the decision!

It was some donkey. The donkey looked at his new owner and was scared. But who was more scared, the donkey or the boy? The boy was proud that he had paid so little. The donkey was good-looking, clean, nice. Its two ears stood up listening to everything. Its eyes were dark eyes like the boy's. When the donkey made on the block, the boy had to clean it up. He couldn't just leave it on the street. No one else had a donkey—or a cow or chickens.

It was soon time to go to Inecik. The boy had to pull him. The donkey pulled the boy, the boy pulled the donkey. The boy had to provide food for him. Watermelon, not the watermelon itself but the skins, the rind. There were plenty on the street because they used to throw the rinds on the street. The children didn't have to look far. The boy said goodbye to his sister, and his little brother followed him to the corner. The brother couldn't go much further.

On the road back, the boy walked next to the donkey. He got on, he got off. The donkey ate some grass. The journey wasn't shorter. It was longer.

When they arrived finally the boy was flushed with excitement and tired from the long walk. His mother said, why did you bring this? What do you need this for? But she was glad her son had arrived safely. She treated him like a king, her heart swelling with relief. But now they had the donkey, what would they do with it? No one stole in the village. They could tie him up outside their hut and he was there all night. A lot of boys came to see the donkey. It was an attraction, something new from these city people, a donkey, something they understood.

Inecik, 1916 (III)

HE AND HIS MOTHER walked the four hours to and from Rodosto many times, replenishing their dry goods to peddle to the farmhouses in Inecik, and letting the donkey carry on his back the bread, eggs, and wheat they brought back to their family in Rodosto. Once, his little sister was with them at their Inecik store in the small concrete hut. He told her to stay at the hut and not to move even a single bit while he and his mother finished the round of a few farmhouses with their wares. She was too small to walk far, and he told her it was better for her to stay put in the hut where no harm could come to her.

But later people ran to find them. The girl had been bitten—was it by dogs or by geese?—on the inside of her leg, and was screaming. It had been a lonely wait for the girl in the hut, and she had amused herself long enough lying looking up at the moving leaves of the tree behind the hut; then she had gone around to the front to see if her brother was back yet. The blood was streaming from the inside of one leg when the frightened mother returned to her child and stopped the bleeding by applying flour that they had in a bin. The child stopped sobbing in terror, and held on to her mother. First she talked about the three geese that had waddled by, and how she had wanted to play with them and imitate their way of walking with their necks long and stretched high, and then she talked about a dog that came out of the bushes to attack her.

This business of being a shop owner in a village with no stores had its flashes of fear that snapped the boy back to reality, and guilt, that if there were no war, and their father were with them, and their uncles and aunts and cousins, they would not have gone bartering for food this way, but would have gone back to dancing class, and kept their straight-backed chairs as elegant partners in time to the music, for that was how they practiced in their Rodosto ballroom dancing class until the food ran out.

The people in the countryside were generous. In exchange for a piece of colorful fabric, they said take some eggs, and no one seemed to care if they took three or eight, as much as they could carry. These farm people weren't busy with counting—take some wheat, they said, pointing out back to the pile of it in the yard. It took a while to understand that the produce had been plentiful this year, and the peasants were busy with harvesting, not with parsing out one little thing or another. At first, before the harvest, the boy had run and hidden and found a bread of pressed hay being fed to the horses. It assuaged his hunger although he felt strange after it. Nonetheless he took some and put it in his shirt to bring to his sister, because she was very hungry also. On good days they had real bread which was very hard, so they put some vinegar in an old can they'd found and dipped the stale bread in the vinegar and that was dinner. The boy and his sister would share. They would ask their mother, do you want any, and she would say "No, I already ate."

On one of their first days in Inecik, in exchange for some buttons and fabric, a woman went inside her kitchen. Perhaps she had seen him around the back trying to feed himself on the horse's hay-cakes. That was the woman who gave them the pot of honey and couldn't have astonished the boy more if she had walked out with the moon placed softly on a dish, ready to carry home for its milky glow. That's what she wanted to pay him with, if it was all right with the boy and his mother. The mother sent her son to bring it to Rodosto.

Only one time he got trouble from a man on his roof. The boy was up on the roof too and was going to get some wheat the man told him he could take. The boy saw a little sand, and told the man, "This wheat is full of sand." What happened then, the boy thought, shouldn't happen to a dog. The roof was on a slant. It was a huge roof with sections and sections of wheat. The man was big. All the boy said was "Look at the sand you have here." The boy didn't finish speaking. The man slapped him, he smacked him down off the roof to the ground. His mother was frightened and angry. She took the boy, and said, "Let's go back to him." She bawled out the man, she was not afraid. The man told her why he hit her son. It was God's wish that the wheat have a little sand in it. "We are lucky to have it," he said.

Often the men let him and his sister help out on the farms, big farms spread out beneath a big sky as if God had planned and planted the earth here in the days of creation. First the people picked the wheat, cutting it with scythes close to the ground, and tying it up into big bundles. The wheat stayed drying out in the sun, day after day, as if there were no hurry in life when you knew what you were doing. The wheat bundles lay out in the big hot fields for weeks. Then they would have to take the wheat kernels out of the straw. You sit on the threshing cart pulled by a horse and you'd ride for three or four hours. The bundles would be loaded up on the cart and as you dumped the stalks the chaff would fly away all day long for days and days and days, the same thing day in and day out. The boy and his sister rode around in the cart eating watermelon. Everyone was riding around in these carts, it was like a party that went on for days in the bright sunshine, that made you forget there was ever such a thing as war. Then you could fill your bag with wheat. The donkey would carry the wheat back to their hut, where the pile in the corner grew higher and higher. The children of the town would come to the store to buy buttons, pay with wheat. All right, fill up a bag with wheat. The mill was always running. The boy would take a bag of wheat. Whoever came to the mill could use it. You poured the wheat through the funnel that was there, and the flour came out on the other side and you picked it up. Sometimes the boy's sister came with him. His mother would say over and over, "Don't fall, you'll trip into the wheels and hurt yourself," but the boy never fell, and his sister stayed back and never fell either. They brought the flour home to their mother in the hut. There were no regrets. The mother took the flour and made it into bread at the fireplace, and the eggs she would cook there too. The family huddled together. When there was bread they divided it. When it was only a little, his mother said, "I don't need it." When they were riding one night on a wagon, and bandits stopped them, all they had was their rusty can with vinegar, so there was nothing to steal. The driver was a kind man, Tajuk, and he said "*Korkma, korkma,*" don't be afraid.

On the road with his donkey, the boy got thirsty and found a little waterfall on a small stream at the side of the road. He knew to drink carefully, watch out for leeches! Sometimes in the summer he would pass a farm growing melons or watermelons. You had to be very careful because you were not allowed to steal. Still when the road was hot and long and endless, a small melon the size of a big man's hand would save him, and he could give the rinds to his donkey.

One day at Inecik the donkey wasn't eating, and the boy began to worry. Usually the donkey needed nothing. It had plenty to eat all day long and whenever a farmer would give them something, the donkey could carry it home. In one day, they could go back and forth from Inecik to Rodosto. But now, the boy asked his friends, what could be the matter? Why won't the donkey eat anything, or even drink water from the stream. A child who said maybe it was a leech, opened the donkey's mouth, and looked. A big leech in the donkey's mouth, on the upper palate, was right there. The boy didn't know how to get it out, but his friends knew. About four or five boys held the donkey, while another opened the donkey's mouth and propped a corncob inside to hold it open. One of the boys took some salt in his hand, stuck his hand in and pulled out the leech. After that the donkey could eat.

One day the donkey wouldn't move. They had left Rodosto, and were still near the city. The donkey lay down right where he was in the middle of the road and couldn't be prodded to get up. The boy was out of his wits with anger and frustration. Finally he decided to get some hay, and light a fire under him. The boy always had plenty of matches, and cajoling the donkey in first sweet and then angry tones did nothing to move him, so the boy lit a small fire near the belly of the donkey. The donkey was extremely nonchalant. He didn't get excited. The donkey stood himself up and walked a step away and then lay down again facing away from the small bundle of burning hay, while the boy sweated in exasperation. A soldier and some fine ladies came by in a cart, and decided to help out. They pulled the donkey a little while, then it sat down, and the elegant party decided to move on and leave the boy in his dilemma. The boy knew he had met his match, because he and the donkey were equally stubborn, and everyone knows stubbornness is one of the hardest things in the world to defeat. So the boy gave up and sat down next to his donkey with respect for something that was more surefooted than the war itself, than he as a salesman selling cloth or buttons, than he as a Jewish son of a Jewish mother, than his hunger when he was hungry and the gaping hole in his stomach would not relent, than his father when he said it was not safe to come back to the family because the Turkish army would nab him and he would be dead. The boy and the donkey sat in the road in silence, not saying a word or a grunt to each other. The sky was as big as the sea or the world or the endlessness of men's desire to live. At a certain point the donkey decided he was ready to get up, and eventually they arrived back in Inecik.

But in the end he gave the donkey to a farmer in Inecik and the farmer gave him five large bags of wheat. That made the pile of the wheat to the ceiling in their hut. It was fall, when the air was getting cooler, and the boy decided this was his moment to be a part of the Hebrew Bible, to make a caravan and return to the city. He had to go because otherwise the wheat would spoil. So now the boy loaded up a cart that he rented with his mother and his sister and all the wheat and two donkeys he borrowed that he loaded down with wheat, and they began the long trek to Rodosto. He watched carefully to make sure no one stole anything from him. His head was filled with the caravan of Joseph's brothers leaving Egypt, and the bag that was opened where a silver cup was found. This story was different and the same; it was scrambled the way a dream scrambles the characters, so that he was Joseph leading the caravan, and Joseph knowing he would be reunited with his family, and Joseph knowing he had to keep thinking and planning, and Joseph outside the city and Joseph inside the city when he arrived, and the weeping of the brothers' reunion. His mind was peopled with Joseph's triumph as the animals carted the wheat to market in Rodosto, a stately and unobstructed caravan. At market the men were shocked by the abundance, and insisted on opening every sack to be sure the wheat was good. Within an hour the boy sold it all. The boy had money now, better than a donkey, better than a store, better than food the need of which rose and fell, as good and triumphant as dance lessons, *un deux trois,   dort besh alti*. Did Joseph take dancing lessons in Egypt

when he was vizier? He knew how not to dance with
the pharoah's wife.

2ND AVENUE SHABBAT, 2001

"ANYONE CAN DRINK IT WITH A SPOON." He was talking about the juice at the bottom of the dessert cup when the cut-up fruit in the elegant cut-glass dish was finished. "Drink the juice, it's the best part," his wife had ordered, because she had made the fresh fruit salad and knew what shouldn't be missed in life. So he saw his opportunity to get a rise out of her. He lifted his dish to his mouth and drank the juice in a gulp. She responded, just as he wanted, teaching him manners, "Can't you drink it with a spoon?"

For some reason the young man on his left at the table had been watching his face when he retorted, "Anyone can drink it with a spoon." The young man was quiet a minute, then broke into gales of laughter at the quiet cleverness of this return. Who was the young man? It must have been a relative, it was his grandson, grown up and well-behaved at the Shabbat table despite the stubble on his chin. The young man had caught his merry twinkle, and now suddenly the young woman at the table burst out laughing too, because it had been such an effortlessly silly yet rebellious statement. For a moment the thrill of making them laugh screwed up his face, as if all were thrown to the winds. He was almost weeping with the thrill of it.

He had never been able to tell jokes, perhaps because he knew the perfect narrative of charm and interaction for selling insurance, and a joke had a different path entirely. In a joke the teller became victorious, pushed himself up in a spiral for surprise and power that left nothing to be done by the listeners except admire the joke teller and swim through the waves, the bursting pleasure of laughter; whereas in the insurance sale, he would lie low and push the listener up to a point of power and desire for more power, which he would then sell to him.

But now suddenly, with nothing left to sell, he had the tone just right and his grandson kept erupting into laughter at the silliness of "Anyone can drink it with a spoon." It must have been his grandson, because before the meal the young man had handed him the prayer book, when at first he said he couldn't do the prayers. The grandson had opened the page for him, and sung "*Yom Ha Shishi*" with him, until rippling into gear he outshot the young man and knew very well who he himself was, the man who had grown up in Turkey and learned as a boy to read Hebrew at a good strong pace, singing out the prayer at a clip. So he himself knew who he was and that was the most important part, what was not to be missed in life. Nothing mattered more than that, not that he was a hundred years old, and a hundred percent dependent on his wife and her two helpers, or that he had a daughter and she was sitting there too, or that it was Shabbat with candles, which his wife had disdain for, or tolerance, as the mood suited her.

He was the perfect clown the rest of the evening. Now that he had hit it right and had an audience with him for every line, he let his eyes twinkle and when his wife wanted him to lift the cane over his head ten times (they would count in French, of course), he mischievously counted the down stroke as well as the up, so that the *un deux trois quatre cinq six sept huit neuf dix* only gave him five cane lifts instead of ten. The next exercise was punching the air, as if you were punching someone very mean. This was against his good-humored character, whereas his wife, for the fantasy of it at any rate, could not imagine anything more pleasurable than punching someone in the face, so she was punching away, getting her own exercise, left right left right, while at the same time scorning him, curling her lip with disgust at his temerity, and baring her teeth at him. "It's somebody very mean, now punch him hard."

The next trial was to get him to stand up from his chair, at the count of *trois*. When his wife got up to *deux* and called on the beat of three, "Now stand up!" he quipped, "you're only up to *deux*," again eliciting gales of laughter from his grandson and daughter because his timing was so good. This was sheer hopeless retaliation and fun and resistance. No pretense now, that he was going to sell you insurance and win money and glory in another way.

But the best was the last, the long walk down the long narrow hallway from their apartment past the elevator all the way to the apartment at the end of the hall. It was a little expedition, everyone singing the *"Marseillaise,"* he with the walker, his wife right behind him pushing the wheelchair should he suddenly need it. *Allons enfants! Marchons!* The bloody flag raised, *formez vos bataillons*. To subvert the walking plan, he kept trying to sit down suddenly in the wheelchair. His wife even spanked him when he tried to sit, pushing his behind and threatening him that he'd be a cripple and she'd leave him if he didn't walk. Finally two thirds of the way back he managed to sit in the chair and decisively end the walking task back to the apartment. Finally his wife said, "All right, you're punishing yourself," and then, "all right, then" in a small huff, she took the walker to bring back into the apartment while his daughter wheeled him. That's when he said to his wife as she guided the walker in front of him, "Walk faster, walk faster." But the Shabbat wine and the candles and the long prayer he had sung had put them all in good spirits, even his wife, so even the walk down the narrow windowless hall past the silent closed apartment doors of those with no family or singing had an air of an adventure satisfactorily completed.

110TH STREET AND 5TH AVENUE, 1920

HE SAW THAT ON SUNDAYS, Italian families bought balloons for their children. The families walked the few blocks to the park and in front of the stone wall under the shade of the trees, bought a balloon for each child. They didn't just buy for one child; they bought for them all. He stood and watched. This was a different country. He couldn't go talk to his mother's cousin, he had nothing to sell, no one to sell it to, there were no mosques, no cafés, and no one was selling trousers door to door, or eggs or wheat. A small church on the corner was very different from a mosque; nobody went there five times a day, and it was closed and empty most of the time. It was lonely in the apartment at the top of a tenement in a sea of five-story stone buildings in the hot city on Lexington Avenue at 112th Street, each building with a fire escape set on its face like a crooked iron mask. He had sung "*Samiotisa*" all the way across the ocean, goodbye to the girl he was leaving behind, a Greek song of longing and farewell. But the girl was no girl, rather his childhood of melons, donkeys, lettuce on a stoop, a caravan of carts of wheat, the countryside, the sky wildly open to breezes from the sea, and the men like his father in fezes saying prayers in Hebrew, all traded in for what—for being a nobody on cluttered hot tenement streets lined along cement pavements, buildings packed with families on each floor, speaking languages he didn't know.

The balloon man spoke Greek, which the boy knew, so he could watch, and charm the details out of him, casually, admiringly, about the $25 tank which the boy then would lug up the four flights to his apartment where he was living with his brothers and sisters, and a one-dollar gross of balloons, and where to get these supplies. The boy wouldn't need English, which he didn't have, just the words, *ten cents.*

So he blossomed like a young balloon tree on the perfect spot he found, uptown from the Greek, on the corner of 110th Street and 5th Avenue, five blocks from his home. He blew the balloons up in the apartment, carried them down the four flights and set himself up in business, watching for the Italian families who came right up to him. He was the man they wanted, the American balloon man, to make a happy day for the family. He had figured out a way to be a breadwinner because he and his brother and sisters in the small apartment needed money, and their parents had been stopped from coming here. He and his sisters played with the baby of his married brother and sang French songs until "*Chantons Victoire*" from the story of Judah Maccabee became an empty chant rather than the call to triumph it needed to be. And how many times would playing with the one-year-old and teaching him to count in French be enough? There was no money in it. The boy's father was still in Turkey. With the balloons, the boy felt a rush of hope. But he said nothing. He kept his mouth shut, collecting dimes. He kept his eyes alert, starting early in the morning, carrying the heavy helium tank up the four flights, blowing up thirty balloons, rushing down the stairs with them, selling them in a flustered panic, dashing the five blocks home, rushing up the stairs, getting thirty more balloons, leaving behind his money, his cap always firmly on his head giving him dignity in the midst of all this dashing and determination like in a movie reel.

It was Sunday, one o'clock in the afternoon. With so many people, could he lose? It was a real day for the park. He was hungry. He figured he'd sell what he had and then go home and eat. A crowd of people was waiting to buy balloons from him. He was standing there, pulling a red balloon out from the bunch, when a policeman came over. What did the man want? Why did the man grab him and pull him down the street? At the precinct no one understood Spanish and they put him in a wagon. He was riding three quarters of an hour. His balloons were dying. "Everybody Out!" He didn't know where he was. "No speak English." Nobody spoke Spanish, French, Greek. Nobody spoke Turkish, Hebrew. The words of all the languages he knew fell away from him. He was worried about the balloons, they were shrinking up. The police put him in a building, they put him in a room and locked him in. He was inside with a half dozen people. He was only in the country three, four weeks. What did he do wrong? He was crying. He was losing money. If he took the air out of the balloons, they would be no good. It was already five, six o'clock, he hadn't eaten lunch, hadn't eaten supper.

The judge didn't come in until ten o'clock at night. The boy was more worried about the balloons than he was about himself. He had his cap, his hat. The policeman said, "Come with me." He was in front of the judge, and a policeman was yelling at him. What was going on? A man came over and slapped him on his head. His hat went a mile away in the huge room. Now he ran after the hat—all he was worried about was the hat. What did the judge say? Maybe it was something about the hat. The boy didn't know, but then suddenly he was outside, on a trolley, first one, and then when he saw it was going in the wrong direction, another, until he got home to his brothers and his sisters.

"Don't worry," they said, when he told them what had happened, his future taken from him in one miserable day. He wanted to go home to Turkey, his friends were there, and the breezes from the sea. "So don't sell on 5th Avenue," they told him, guessing. He didn't know, he didn't read signs. And he had no regrets, even on the ship when he put his head through the porthole, he didn't take off his hat. He had put his hand on his hat and it stayed put and with his face out in the middle of the sea everything was beautiful.

Murray Hill, 1924

THE RULE WAS: you must wait two weeks before you were allowed to sell your first policy! It was too long, but in from the sharp December wind, he cheerfully greeted the white-shirted man in the tiny white marble booth at the base of the spiral staircase, and the man remembered him from their talk a few days before about this rich solid sixteen-story building at 26th Street and Broadway. "The man in the booth will buy a policy from me," the young man thought to himself as he started up the spiral marble staircase to the third floor.

To have a spiral staircase in the place he worked! Can you beat that! The building was white and prosperous looking, older than he was. The flat-faced clock perched atop the small marble booth showed blandly that he was early. That man had to sit all day in that little booth, the newly hired insurance man thought. He himself had had enough of sitting at the skirt factory just a few blocks away, in the red bricked-in factory district, the bricks left over from when the Jews were slaves in Egypt, mortared dark red bricks, closing him in as he sat at the sewing machine hour after hour, attentively steering the cloth, judging the dangerous needle, alternating impatience with calm. Hadn't his mother sung while she sewed—but no one sang in the rows of machines humming here. His brother who set up the factory with him hadn't thought about all this sitting, but his brother had his own problems. For him, however, to get out the factory door was like breaking out of prison, to stride down the street a whole man, feel his arms and legs in motion, his back useful and strong, his steps to the subway brisk, his curiosity stirred up and alive with interest in each building he passed, each bricked-in factory where old machines and young lives hummed and droned with a desperate optimism.

It wasn't just the walking down the street, but the people he wanted. All those people locked in and locked out, in each one a desire like his, for life.

And now, on his second week of work as he entered the office from the three-flight spiral staircase, its spiraled railing polished dark rich wood, and vases of fresh flowers set in small alcoves along the wall as if this were the Garden of Eden—in mid-December— as he entered this broad, open, machine-free spread of desks and tables, he knew he was home. He would sell.

He had sold women scarves and fabric, now he would sell them something else. What were women but mothers, determined their children would survive, intent on facing down every threat. If a prospect didn't have his own mother's courage, he knew she wanted it. He talked to women with respect, even if he had learned a trick from his cousin in Rodosto that made the women think the colors on the fabric would not run. His sense that he had found work that was meant for him dawned on him in those first two weeks when he was told he would canvass in apartment houses, brownstones, and tenements each day. Now finally he understood the New York City architecture of buildings, each building packed with apartments, each apartment packed with families. The grim spelling of all those buildings lining the streets was nothing less than a chance to sell to each and every apartment. You didn't need a mosque or a marketplace, or the countryside or a smoky café. The grid of stacked apartments and myriads of doors up and down the stairs was a grid of desire and possibility. He laughed when he realized what he had not understood before. The tenements, like uptown where he lived, were not in the way, they were the way.

The company gave him literature, piles of four-by-six booklets with covers colored like candies, cherry red, pineapple yellow, lime green, with advice as clear as good arithmetic or stories. He looked through them. He was instructed to give these cheerful health booklets as gifts to every prospect he visited. The company had helped patients with TB, and worked with settlement houses; then a man at the Home Office (his name sounded Jewish!) had started the booklet distribution program. But the new agent didn't need proof or science or a company history. The booklets were just right. He had never had samples to give away, to prove himself a serious man, the way the universe was giving and generous with its fruits of the earth. Now he would be a provider, helping women by helping men be providers. At his office now, he barely saw the other men at this training meeting, but thought about the people he would sell to and serve. The company only stood to gain by helping their policy-holders prevent illness, bring a child through sickness, help a husband with a disability. The company's nursing service would come to a policy-holder's home at any time of day or night. They were serious. Everyone and the company stood to gain by health, hygiene, caring, and welfare, so it was simple arithmetic, the easiest arithmetic of common sense. It added up.

What confused him was the manager's talk about "standards," expectations to "place" a certain amount each week. He couldn't even hear the number. Does a man need to be told to eat every day? Or to breathe and count his breaths? That would be confusing. Counting would put the numbers on the wrong basis. Desire was what he had instead. He could step aboard, like on a train, for whole stretches, ten or twelve hours at a go.

The words *industrial* and *ordinary*, two different kinds of insurance, lit up a magical sense of possibilities for him. He understood them immediately. Industrial insurance was for those at the bottom, eating heads of lettuce during a famine—that was industrial— while the other insurance was for those who had seen the light of day and always knew there would be food on the table—that was ordinary. Those on the bottom could do weekly deposits, a few cents a day. Those at a higher level would pay four premiums a year, or two, or one. And premiums was a fine word, bringing to mind the best prizes; you would be prized if you prized your family well enough to secure their future against loss.

Selling industrial to people scraping by was like creating a burial society for the whole city. Every immigrant knew that you needed to be able to pay for the burial of family members. Burial gave meaning to the terrible losses that hung over your head. With the worry of burial off your mind you could take one day at a time. One man opened his window and threw a pail of cold water on him and another rookie for daring to mention death even in this most sensible way, but most people wanted to know that this frightening thing was taken care of, so selling policies insuring everyone from the first day to the seventieth year, infant, child and adult of both sexes, no medical examinations required, and letting them cover this vast burial cost week to week was like selling everyone a solid pair of shoes that fit well for a good price; how could you go on without them? A salesman performed a service.

You didn't *say* the word industrial, but it meant the world to him, industrious, industry, the whirring engines of economic opportunity, a chance to move up to the grand plateau of ordinary, at which you could breathe. You had ventured, you had achieved, you could sit at the table, you had a job or a business or your family did, you could deal in an ordinary manner. Everyone certainly wanted that. Millions of people had come to New York for precisely that.

Now the door of the United States was closed to immigrants; this year the gate was shut. But if you'd made it here by now, you had a great wild sensation. The young man felt it all around him.

Monday Tuesday Wednesday Thursday Friday, Monday Tuesday Wednesday Thursday Friday. On Saturday he sold his first two policies, ordinary, to himself for $3000 and his brother, locked in his skirt factory, for $1000. *Baruch Ata Adonai, elohenu melech haolam, shehechianu, vekiyemanu, vehigianu, lazeman hazeh,* he had reached the season of his first real sale in America.

MURRAY HILL, 1925

A MAN FROM THE HOME OFFICE wanted to take his picture for the company's glossy magazine. What was he now, a star, because selling was candy to him? Eight months, and he led the entire country in sales. Was that a surprise? The Home Office magazine man must be paid a lot because he took his time. He posed the agent in his three-piece suit and new hat coming up—on his way up—literally and figuratively from a just-below-street-level apartment and having opened the ornate, waist-high black iron gate of a fancy brownstone with curved stone carvings and luxuriant ivy trailing from a window box above and just behind his head. The agent was to hold a small stack of welfare booklets, so that you could see the two human figures in a sketch on the cover against his knee, so he would have a look at once physical and intellectual vigor. It wasn't his photograph in a jacket too small for him for the ship manifest to America; it was the whole of him, a man well dressed—you could even see a bit of the sole of his shoe as he stepped up from the top basement step to street level; he looked tall and handsome in this full page photo that would be given the first listing in a glossy table of contents swirling with calligraphy. The photograph of him would get a whole separate listing from the article about him, the editor said, because he wanted to give agents' wives a husband for their husbands to emulate in their own eyes, and someone whom they would trust opening their door to.

The agent said he wasn't married himself, of course, but all the better, the magazine man said to be friendly. But how should the agent look for the camera? "Look serious and purposeful but at the same time as if you care about people."

"I do care about people," the agent said and laughed. He thought, I don't care about cameras or pictures. The magazine man didn't want the agent's words or thoughts and certainly not a laugh, but the agent had had to break the tension, and at the same time he knew he was wasting his time. He could be out selling. The agent asked the magazine man if he had thought about upgrading his insurance policies, because he would be happy to look them over. Well, of course, this was a college man, and there wouldn't be time for a sale, but perhaps charm would pay off in the end. Usually the agent was doing the selling but now the magazine was selling *him*, and he should be pleased. In fact he pictured his family sitting around the table admiring this "informal photograph" and his mother laughing out loud, "*Bre!*" So when the photographer snapped the picture the agent did look serious but his mouth was a tiny bit pushed to one side, as if his words usually right from his heart had to be squeezed off or clamped down. One hand was on his knee, the other arm hung down and you could see the creases on the jacket sleeve at the elbow. The young agent knew how to have his picture taken, you closed your mouth so that not even a fly could go in. But the magazine man said, "Yes, be serious but show on your face you're congratulating yourself because you have sold a policy and protected a family. You are serious and care about everything that is important in life—but don't try to look friendly—it's not suitable." The magazine man cocked the brim of the agent's new felt hat the slightest bit for jauntiness and tilted the agent's face the slightest bit in the opposite direction for balance. The location for the photo shoot was selected from a wealthy block in the territory, but the sleeve creases and ascent from below street level capitalized on how the 1920s saw upward mobility in every angle in this athletic young Turk's (what the hell kind of name is that) candid pose with, in spite of all cash values, dreamy eyes peering out at the woman flipping through the glossy magazine to better gauge her own breadwinner's daily work. The magazine, of course, was pitched to the insurance agents, the field force, but how better to get to them than through their wives?

Madison Square, 1926

"In the first place I try to draw out in the prospect the desire for insurance." That's what he told the reporter who called for an interview. But the agent needed to plan how to explain what he meant; he stayed up until twelve the night before to write down his thoughts in English and get them straight. Selling meant you had something that people wanted. Insurance was not just something you sold for people to wear or to use to smoke (and while away an afternoon in frustration), but something important that would make a person feel organized and secure. It was thrift and protection. It let you put a value on a life, so that it had meaning, the way planting a row of trees along the edge of a field gave a field meaning, and definition. The desire of the client chimed in with his own desire to be there with the right product and the right price, thought the agent, but he wouldn't say all that to the reporter, since it was too obvious. Of course the reporter knew the agent wanted to sell. Doesn't every agent want to sell as much as he can?

The main thing was the literature. He always carried welfare literature with him, to give to prospects. The company wanted him to take piles of the booklets; this approach, amazingly in tune with his own goals, to make the best of life, be healthy and energetic and forward-thinking, couldn't have suited him better.

He lavished moments on the booklets' helpful tips on how to stay healthy and guide one's family to hygiene and well-being. He'd never had something to give away as a child, except his sincerity—he'd had to charge for every needle and button. That was why he was able to impress on his clients that these booklets were to be treasured. They weren't what you'd expect, a piece of advertising from the company, but useful tips on fever, or how to know when to go for a doctor, or how to teach a child to wash his hands. He always carried the literature with him, and said the booklets were to be cherished, not thrown away. Each booklet conveyed hope and education, the best of all possible connections for people up and down in each building.

Canvassing apartments on every floor, he would work his way up the stairs in a building, then to save time, go up to the roof and step over the roof edge to the next building, then work his way down, landing by landing, then enter the next building, work his way up, over, down, up the next, over the roof and down. He spread out his two-block territory (they called it a debit) over four days and got to know people rather than rushing through in a day and a half. The reporter didn't want to put that in about the roof tops, understandably; what the reporter liked was the agent's offhand comment that he didn't bother about the standards suggested by the company, like writing a certain number of sales a week, or each week increasing his sales by so much. For one thing, the agent said, those standards were much too low, like telling a woman she could only sew twenty skirts a week when she had a family to feed. Numbers were distracting and would have hemmed him in; adding up his numbers would have taken time away from selling. The reporter was interested, and surprised and asked, "Well, what is your standard—how much do you try to sell a week?" "I'm so glad you asked that," said the young agent, who spoke sometimes as if he were reading a haggadah of insurance. "My only standard is the number of hours in a day, and how long I can keep going. Even if I set my own numbers, they'd just slow me down too because I'd be thinking about numbers, not people. Instead I just keep going, no matter how much I've sold. The reporter wrote this up as a headline, "HIS ONLY STANDARD IS HIS CAPACITY FOR WORK" and then added "The power to raise his salary is always his." In Turkey that power had been less than meager, because the empire was dying. Here he could make money, and that's what he wanted to do. The reporter wrote that up crisply, and it sounded professional and masculine, especially with the agent's selling statistics for his first six months showing that he led the entire United States in the business, the way Babe Ruth led in home runs. Way out in front. The reporter didn't say that, but mentioned the agent spoke six languages plus English and always answers his prospects in their own languages. The article said not every agent could be a linguist but many with "foreign" territories might be wise to pick up a "smattering of phrases" to feel at home as the company's representative in a city packed with immigrants. The reporter did not understand that the agent did not deal with a smattering of phrases, but the poetry of hope. The agent had been sifting languages all his life with the carnival of peoples, his neighbors. The Jews were a tiny minority compared to other groups—Greeks, Armenians, Turks—and brokered their way through the day like boys darting through crowds on a holiday. That reporter must have been paid a lot because he put together a fine article contrasting perfectly good standards that other agents used to sell impressive amounts of insurance, with what this agent used, the number of hours in a day that he could keep going, his appetite for people and their interest in a product that could change their lives. The reporter didn't put it in the article but the agent's eyes were not bigger than his stomach. His eyes were big, his hunger was big, but he was making up for centuries, and he liked people in this country. They were like him. They were ready for a better life. *Bre!*

THE EAST COAST, 1927

THE NIGHT BEFORE SPEAKING to the writer from the East Coast insurance field newspaper, he sat up late at the kitchen table, the fire escape outside the window, his noisy family finally sleeping, the smell of onion and romano cheese *mantis* rich in the air. The headline would call him a star because he sold more small policies with small premiums than anyone in the United States. It was good to take the time to get it right, to figure out his step-by-step approach with the prospect. He was no longer collecting premiums; time spread out in front of him like a big table. The Scottish manager had promoted him to Assistant Manager. Now like a doctor doing rounds, he took the others with him. They saw the way he stacked the literature to bring it along. They saw how he drew the prospect in. He liked people and understood their needs. Good grooming, he would say, a serious and purposeful manner, an organized approach all paid off. Each day he made a list of the cold calls and interviews for the next day. No bit of work was too insignificant. Always ask clients, he told himself and the others, for referrals, and find out about the people, their work, their families. It was almost too easy. So you're prepared when you meet them. Don't think it's a waste of time to go to an entirely different part of the city. It's a chance to canvass every single apartment in that new building in another neighborhood. The agent had so much to say, he didn't want to overload the writer. Keep it focused. I draw her in. Here's a pamphlet. The company cares. We have a nursing service. If you have a policy you can have a nurse in any time someone in your family is ill. But you need to give me your name, and height and weight. Don't assume I can get you a policy until I tell you. Let me look into it for you. If I can, I'll bring you a form. You'll get something in the mail. Two weeks later, I offer congratulations and the form. The company will contact you in fifteen days and you'll get a premium receipt book. You should make your deposits (don't call them payments, no one likes to pay, but they do like to save) ten weeks at a time— make them in advance if you can—because that way you can feel secure that your policy will stay in force. Five weeks would be fine. I don't usually work in the evenings, but if the head of the household would like to take the time to meet with me, I'll come by at a time you say. When I meet with him, I'll tell him he's the one with the responsibilities of the family on his shoulders, and I have something worthwhile to present to him. I'll be brief, I'll write the sale, my manager is pleased, so am I. Keep the story simple for the writer, and for the prospect. It works because everyone wants it to work. The man wants his evening back, although he finds it interesting, and this man from Turkey is really something. The man wants his wife appeased, his value as a worker validated with numbers. This business is on the cusp of something important that everyone wants and needs in a city of millions, a city in the twentieth century. People want to value themselves, and I help them. The agents I take around like it too. I give them this or that sale to show them how easy it is, like the pamphlets. It's easy if there's something to give, and if there's a lot I can give, the whole thing moves forward. Everyone benefits. The sky is the limit. The agents are inspired. That's what I'll do. I'll ask the reporter if he'd like me to review his policies.

So why did they close the door to America? The new assistant manager went to bed, ready for a full and promising next day. In a famous museum some blocks away, empty-eye-socket skulls perched on a bookcase were used to tell a less promising story, of eugenics, a dank false science that would lock millions of people in the years to come into Europe's mass-murder killing fields. The Turkish young man slept well, on the cusp of acceptance, not knowing a thing. He was making his way in America.

Long Beach, 1973

HE SITS AWKWARDLY on the depressed edge of the bed that is his wife's side because that's where the telephone is, on the night table, a large grey plastic telephone like an old Cadillac, with a large transparent plastic dial in the middle.

"Good morning, Morris," he says and says who's calling, his list from the synagogue with some scribbled notes in his lap, his glasses on, his phone personality in gear, organized, focused, happy to be doing what he loves.

"I have a proposition for you."

Morris must crack some joke because they share masculine laughter, brotherly or avuncular laughter as if they go way back and can count on each other to be warm and receptive.

"You know if it's me calling it's a good one." He smiles again, pleased at his segue. When you're talking on the phone, smile. They can hear it through the telephone wires.

"Well, you do it every year, so you might as well get it done now. I'll take care of it and it will be off your list.

"What do you stand to gain? Well, I'll tell you if you do a double page this year, you'll gain even more."

Again, affable laughter. "You of all people I don't have to tell."

He was right. Of course, Morris knew: he'd be supporting the synagogue, he'd end up contributing anyway, why not have the social standing of being a major contributor, it spoke well of his success as a lawyer, it would help sell other ads, it would please his wife—she'd enjoy the dinner dance more than usual, be proud and satisfied.

"How's your beautiful wife, Eve?" the caller said to take the pressure off by changing the topic before Morris made a decision, although he also knew how Morris's mind worked.

Morris was a busy man, and needed to get to other calls. "Let's do it," he said. "Great. You're really something. I knew when my secretary said it was you, I didn't stand a chance."

More affable laughter. Morris said his wife would write up the ad, put the whole family in, and drop it off.

The caller put down the phone, checked the list, was thinking about who was next. It was always good to get rolling with a big one.

"Are you going to be on the phone all morning?" his wife asked barging into their bedroom, annoyed at daylight (or evenings) spent on the phone. "Because I thought we'd do some shopping."

He was like a kid reading a comic, being interrupted and told to do his homework.

He immediately translated his goal into his wife's terms: "I only have to sell six more ads and we're set for the dinner dance." She hated spending money on the expensive tickets for the dinner dance, but she also hated his geared-up telephoning, especially because he was so good at it and enjoyed it so much. So it was a difficult choice about what to be most irritable about, the prospect of his pleasure on the phone, or the prospect of having to shell out $300 apiece for the tickets. It took too much effort to decide, and like Morris, she knew she didn't stand a chance, so there was no point arguing with him. Unlike with Morris, there was no affable laughter. "For Christ's sake, you never know when to stop," she contented herself with venting her exasperation angrily and setting him on edge. He was supposed to be retired, but it was endless. She went outside on the patio to study the bridge column.

She did love the dinner dance. He'd wear a tuxedo, she her long grey gown, they'd take a picture. Her husband was an excellent dancer, they both were, and when they danced they were a couple everyone commented on, the tango, the rhumba, the mambo. They didn't have to talk. They were a handsome couple. The band's music would sweep through the hall. He liked that too.

Topkapi Restaurant, 1981

IT WAS ONE OF THOSE expensive East Side restaurants that are small and dark on a sunny winter day, as if there were something rich about thick white tablecloths set out on small tables protected from the onslaught of common sunlight. It was his niece's idea—she'd heard the food was excellent, and so the celebration crammed the group close together.

Perhaps the expense of it, and that his niece had suggested the restaurant, took his wife off the hook and allowed her to let go. She could be celebrating him instead of berating him. Of course, it was more than that, it was the achievement and immense relief about the daughters, all married now. But she wasn't thinking about their married daughters now; she just let go as if doing so was an entirely novel and appealing idea. "Tell them the story of the dimes," she said, with a dramatic burst of pride, after her toast on the wine, ending in *"y tiempo para gozarlo"*— and time to enjoy it!

It was his birthday, and it would be just the thing to allow him a heroic recounting. The floor was his at last. After all, what was impressive about him was part of her story, what she made possible and was part of. What a novel thought, so ordinary, that as a wife she could catch the reflected glory, to brighten up the restaurant, but she hardly ever thought of it, since there was so much to do most of the time to fight his enthusiasm and pleasure and determination. But once in a while, she saw it all in a new light, that it was part of her story.

"Your father," she said for, in addition to the niece, two daughters had come, one with her husband of ten years, "was the best man the company ever had. Did they appreciate him? Did they see what he had done? Of course not, or they would not have forced him to retire, they would have made him a vice president in the national office." She'd always told him what she later read in a big article about the company in the *New York Times*, that they don't promote Jews—why are you giving your life to this company, you should go out on your own. Don't you see the anti-semitism staring you in the face!

"Tell them about the dimes," she repeated as she dipped a crust of bread into the tarama, chased an olive around the plate, savored the smell of grilling fish—and drank the wine, allowing him to say a blessing over it, *Baruch Ata...*

"The dimes," he started.

"It wasn't just the dimes," his wife burst in. "Every time the company had a problem office in New York City, they moved him in there to take over."

Sipping her wine, she expanded on her theme: "Well, that first manager, that Scotsman, before we were married, he knew a good thing. You were selling more insurance than anyone in the country, and you barely spoke English. So he made you an Assistant Manager."

The broiled fish, a whole fish with eye intact, arrived on a platter gloriously decorated with thin lemon slices and Italian parsley sprigs, the skin bristling with flavor and crisp shimmering blackness. He'd wanted porgy, a fish which embodied his whole savoring of life, but quickly adjusted to the fact that an expensive Turkish restaurant wouldn't serve porgy, but striped bass. Neighborhood Greek restaurants served porgy.

"Once they saw how you could lead the men they gave you a whole district of your own, stuck you wherever they needed someone to turn around a chaotic mess, and when you fixed that one they sent you on to another, one office after another. You'd wake up the men. It was as if they were sleeping, or depressed. You'd go in like a whirlwind and stir them up and wake them and bring them to life."

It was something to be proud of! His wife suddenly saw it as something that could bring shine to her life—her husband's success. A tale to tell!

She let him get a word in; he said, "I'd ask them, 'You went to the movies and sat in the dark all afternoon, when you could be making sales?'" He went on, unchecked. "I'd show them how to do it."

He said he took them around, showed them how he sat and talked with people. He knew how from Turkey. "It's like you have all day. I'd get to the sale, but first you need to recognize the people for what they were trying for in life— if you rushed you didn't catch them where you wanted them."

His wife said with a sniff of anger, "He loved every prospect as a friend." That could have sent her veering off jealously, "He tried to give away our daughter's tricycle, he said his client's daughter wanted one, can you imagine, but—"

"My father used to play backgammon with his customers," the niece commented. Everyone at the table knew this; people came from all over South America to play with this master of *shesh besh*, his cigarette dangling from his mouth in the back room of his wildly packed and cluttered basement store.

"First they sent me to New Lots in Brooklyn," he went on. "What could anyone do there? Nothing. The men were as lazy as a bunch of *zazulias*"—the word smacked of Turkey. "But I talked to them. I sat them down. 'So what are you doing,' I asked them. 'Are you in business or not? Are you going to do something with your lives?' They just looked at me as if they had never thought about this. 'I'll show you. Come with me.'

"They didn't know how to sell. First one, then another, I took them with me.

"And they saw it was possible and more than possible. It was the best thing in the world. You sat down with the people. Like we're sitting here today. You talked. You didn't hurry. You get acquainted. And little by little they feel they know who you are, and the next thing, it's so natural. It's like eating pie."

"Pie, when was the last time you ate pie?" his wife interjected. But it was an American thing to say and he relished his American success. Selling was as easy as eating pie. He pulled his arms in against his ribs, the way Ed Sullivan did, to keep his pleasure up.

"I changed the whole place. Then they sent me to a district in the Bronx, the same thing, but worse. More men that did nothing. They sat around the office. They couldn't be bothered. They were as lazy as the day was long. I brought them together. I talked to them. Is this what you want to make of your lives? Nothing? Don't you have wives? Don't you have children? It was like when I had that donkey. First they'd shift to one side. Then the other. What for? They'd never seen someone sell insurance. They had no idea what it was all about. I took them for a walk around the neighborhood. We walked by all the stores. We saw the people working in these stores, stuck there all day. And just waiting for someone to come in and listen as they talked about their children, their hopes and fears, their fears for their future.

"The men had no idea how lucky they were not to be stuck in a store all day. It was like a prison. 'You're free men,' I'd say, grabbing an agent by the collar. 'Harry,' I'd say to the agent, 'you can walk outside in the open air, do you see what this means—the shopkeeper doesn't have that. You're the king, you enter their store and they breathe a sigh of relief, here's a person, you're not stuck like them, sitting duck.'"

"You're very funny," his niece said, "you know that?"

But his wife interjected again, "Yes, *he* wasn't stuck, but I was! Waiting at home every night for him to come home from work."

He plunged ahead. "So after I got those men up and running, they sent me to another office, this one in Flatbush. These men were right with me. We were a team, from the first day. They were going, going, going. Our productivity was tops. But I saw something. The hours were too long and there were too many stairs to climb, day in and day out. Everything was too slow.

"I had an idea." Was the waiter listening? Such a small restaurant. So what? Good. Maybe he'd learn something. They had the restaurant to themselves. But it didn't suit his expansive style, wasn't the right platform, wasn't a big space open to gestures and laughs and a real speech. He wasn't in his element. He wasn't in charge. He was sitting, not standing. He had to act tight—there wasn't room for him to spread his arms, raise his voice in oratory, get the crowd roused to song or admiration. This wasn't a large ship, just a small boat ("three men in a rowboat, no matches, how did they light a cigar?") he had to constrict himself, act dignified in a rich way, keep his arms to his side, stay seated, act the part of a successful man. He looked at his son-in-law to find a groove of appreciation.

"What would you do if the whole style of doing business was climbing stairs, one flight after another, and knocking on doors, ringing doorbells, canvassing day in and day out, long hours of presenting yourself in person, ten hours a day, and you knew in your bones it was just too slow?

"The world was spinning. Were you going to stand still? Let's not even talk about what happened in Europe. But hadn't our honorable men on the beach in Normandy beaten them back? Our country led the fight to save the world!" He avoided unspeakable words, besides, out of respect, one didn't even say the word God, even in Hebrew. One could get pulled down into the hole, pulled through the center of the earth—forget to fight.

"And do you think the Jews stood still? They got their own country! After thousands of years. Can you beat that?" He kept his voice low, circumspect, befitting a small dark expensive restaurant.

"It's the only way!" he said.

"Keep on," he added.

"So I said to the men, 'we're going to do things differently.' I had sent my assistant manager to the bank and there he was right next to me. His pockets were full, and he started emptying them onto the desk.

"What do you think he had?

"He had rolls and rolls and rolls of—dimes.

"'What's going on?' the men shouted, trying to figure it out.

"'Think about it. Think about all that shoe leather. There has to be a faster way,' I told them. 'You have to stay ahead of the competition.' Then I looked from one man to the next.

"'We're going to hit the corner phone booths!' I told them. I took the whole place by surprise. Can you imagine that? Had anyone else ever done it? No! No one!

"And that's what we did. I had my assistant manager make a map of all the phone booths in Flatbush. He assigned each man to a phone booth, and gave him two rolls of dimes. This was the wave of the future. We were on board. And this was only the beginning!"

"What do you mean?" asked his niece. She looked at him with her head tilted, her eyes wide open, her cherry mouth deferential.

"It was over, the era of wearing out our shoe leather or our patience—was over."

His wife said, "Oh, for goodness sake! you have to explain. Tell them what you mean!"

"Instead of ringing door bells, each man would take his dimes and get on the telephone. Hello, you introduce yourself. You smile. You think about the person you're talking to. You're a nice person on the telephone, which anyone would appreciate. You convey your personality, you sell yourself, what you can mean to these people, and if it sounds like it's worth a visit, you arrange that. You'd be amazed. You can't read about these things in Books! It worked, each agent had his assigned corner phone booth, and they spread through the neighborhood to their metal phone booths like wildfire, with their rolls of dimes.

"But then I had a better idea. It didn't take me long." He looked at his family. "Why should the men have to stand in phone booths all day juggling dimes? They loved it, and they laughed, but sometimes the rolls of dimes would tear open, and the bank wondered what was going on, a hundred rolls of dimes at a time.

"The next step was right there, as it always is once you start doing something. I told my assistant manager to call the telephone company and have them install a phone for each man at his desk. 'Who will pay for them, boss?' he asked. 'But boss,' he said, 'they'll be mad! A phone for each man? That's going to cost a lot of money! They'll be furious!' 'Well, then, I'll pay. Don't think about it—get the phones installed.' It was a thing of beauty. The whole office.

A whole long office and on every table a telephone. You've never seen anything like this!"

"And did the company ever find out?" asked his niece. "You're so smart," she added with a laugh.

"The Main Office came around one day. There was the whole office spread like a gymnasium, each man at his desk, each man with a telephone on his desk, each man talking into a telephone. It was the most beautiful thing you could imagine. Each man was making sales, each man was arranging appointments—was selling!

"'What's going on here?' said the man from the Main Office. He'd never seen anything like that. He was furious. 'Who put in those telephones? Get them out of here. We're not going to pay for those phones. Who gave you permission to do that?'

"'I'll pay for the phones.'

"The man from the Main Office left angrily. The men were all busy. They were spread out like gulls riding waves on the sea. In the sunlight.

"I didn't pay those telephone bills. It was a big company. The biggest in the world. I never heard a peep out of them, my office was doing so much business. The men came in and sat down at their desks and got to work. It was like giving them respect, giving them those phones."

He risked a pause.

"And you know what, soon every office in the country had telephones. A sea of telephones. How else would you do business?"

His niece suddenly blurted out, with outrage and awe—"Oh, my God! You invented telemarketing. Oh, no! Don't tell anyone."

"That's good."

"And the Chinese agents you recruited at the Chinese restaurant?" His wife burst in before anyone could finish savoring the dimes. "You got twenty waiters to show up in your office and had the only Chinese agents in the country. No one else thought of it."

"That's another story," he said, keeping up with the bones in his fish. He could have ordered a filet but that would have been a disappointment. The bones lined the edge of the plate when the waiter stepped in to remove it. Soon, rice pudding. He never believed in birthdays. They didn't celebrate them in Turkey. Who even knew when you were born?

THE WALDORF ASTORIA, 1964

THE COMPANY HAD LONG HAD the knack of rewarding their best field men by dazzling their wives. A Waldorf Astoria dinner dance meant tuxedos and modern evening dresses, boutonnières and flower arrangements, the dance floor, the orchestra, prime ribs *au jus*, and the glory of cachet to celebrate these men in the prime of their lives. The Waldorf's Sert Room was perfect. The manager's district had led New York for 1963, and was second in the country! The manager was speaking at the center of the dais, flanked by company officers who knew him as an inspired district leader and salesman, a combination hardly ever seen with such surprising sales points.

"And I want to thank my beautiful wife, for her wonderful support that made all of this possible," said the man in whose honor the whole dinner was being held. He gestured happily to her with his right hand. He had even arranged an escort for one of their daughters—he found a handsome young Egyptian Jew who was a good dancer and would show her a good evening.

His wife was sitting right next to him on the flower-bedecked dais, and she looked sternly beautiful with her hair elegantly coiffed at a beauty parlor earlier that day. Instead of nodding graciously, she called out with anger to the two hundred paired-off men and women attentive to her husband's speech, "He did it in spite of me. I didn't do anything to help him."

Her voice jumped on "in spite" to let everyone know how much spite she felt. It was one of those glitches in a perfect evening that you had to pretend didn't happen, as if in the kitchen a camera had caught one of the waiters doing something shocking to someone's drink. How odd to have an outspoken wife. You couldn't understand women, you simply had to try to make them happy. That had long been the manager's approach. And soon she would be with him out on the dance floor, their posture and footing impeccably right, the most admired couple in the Waldorf Astoria.

He didn't know why the hotel had that name, but he knew John Jacob Astor was once the richest man in the country. Astor's ships to and from China would have been news to the manager—and the opium in the hold—and that Astor cleverly bought land early and held onto it in ways that meant waves of foreclosures during the panics. The honored manager had taken dance lessons for barter in Rodosto during the war, the boys each with a tall-backed chair for a partner. The company vice president gave the manager and his wife the first dance. The tango, sharp-angled and dramatic yet in their hands gracious and calm was the dance the couple liked best. The pleasure for the honored man was that the evening was not just for him, but that on the sea of his enthusiasm and determination, he had lifted the fortunes of all these men in his district, had lifted them to see how much was possible when they recognized their common goal and how they could help each other get there, by pulling together for a district-wide record.

He had been invited to his first Waldorf Astoria dinner in 1925, in his manager's twelfth-floor apartment in the old Waldorf Astoria, dripping in European magnificence, on 34th Street and 5th Avenue. That was a private dinner for the two of them, served at a small round table in the room by white men in white gloves. When he went back to his family's tenement apartment, his sisters, doing piecework embroidery on dolls' dresses, hung on every word about the fabulous world their gangly determined brother, breaking away from the skirt business, was evidently becoming a part of, although it didn't seem like him. Of course that tête-à-tête wasn't really in his manager's "apartment," but a room the company had on tap; but for a Turkish Jew to celebrate his extraordinary first year sales record there meant that he had come to the right country at the right time for the right work, even the right district office right across town from the skirt factory he and his older brother had started for a meager profit amidst all the other garment factories on West 26th Street.

Now, almost forty years later, the invited guests paired off man and woman like in an old-fashioned cotillion in a movie, except without the elaborate French hairdos and floor-length gowns. They filled the dance floor. The manager, his wife elegantly in his arms, was proud that his entire sales force was to be honored at this dinner with plaques, photographs, and speeches. In a year of frenetic and sustained determination, they had snatched victory from other districts once again, and even the clerical staff, those girls in high heels, would be given trophy pins to celebrate their loyal and energetic support.

The waltz now let him swell with pleasure. He *had* been coming home late every night. But ah, that new office, right in the hub of Brooklyn, on Livingston, the building with its mild blue mosaic entrance wall. He was no longer on the outskirts of Brooklyn, far out on Flatbush Avenue, but by his own pluck had opened a new kind of insurance office with thirty hand-picked insurance specialists. It was a new building, a corner building, and nearby were dramatic important buildings with huge Greek revival columns, and the crowning amenity: the subway at Borough Hall. The Lexington Avenue subway could speed him home. It was the same subway as when he'd first come from Turkey and lived uptown on Lexington Avenue. Never mind the elegant Waldorf Astoria, with its luxurious fittings to indulge the women; in his new office, he was right there in the hub, having figured out brilliantly what his next step should be. He had known exactly how to approach the company, and they had given him the green light.

So not only did he have a triumphal dinner with which to reward all his men and their wives, but even better, he had moved almost every single one of them from the outskirts of the borough to a modern centrally located new kind of office.

His wife was in his arms. Her outburst—these were the facts of life, gravity— in the person of a wife, or in the bombs on a city in Turkey—would frighten you, but you danced, you worked, you sold, you spread good cheer, you made jokes, and there you were floating on the blue Danube to the admiration of all, and most of all to the renewed, confirmed optimism of all.

The company had led off the evening with everyone singing "My Country 'Tis of Thee." Then they pitched heartily into "The Star Spangled Banner," and finally, of course, the company anthem. Every man and woman in the splendid room had stood and joined in the resplendent singing.

"This is the most exciting moment in my career," the honored man said at the podium, "because it has been outstanding to work with every single one of you. You have sought to do your best, and we have all learned together that the best is right there to be achieved if we all expect it of ourselves. Nothing can be better than to know that we can actually reach the goals that we have—surprisingly—set for ourselves. I say surprisingly because it took a wild imagination to think that we could outdo every district in New York, when every district has good, honest, determined men, who, like us, care and want the best for their families and for our city as a whole. And yet we took up that wild card, because there it was right in front of us, and why not? Why not read each other our prospecting letters, and keep them going out, one after the other? Why not say just the right thing in those follow-up calls, those words that make prospects respond? Why not be a happy person, a pleasure to do business with? Why not help one another on evenings and weekends to make sure each one of us has the knowledge and the tools and the support of us all to get it right, and so we did." He paused. "And here we are.

"Lifting the prospects of our clients and ourselves, lifting the opportunities for all, and confirming at every turn the possibilities for betterment on every level, we are public servants, and that is the pleasure we get from this celebration and from our work."

The company vice president, listening to the manager, knew what he had in this man. The vice president, like many of his fellow officers, all Christian, was tall and impressive. He was a full head taller than the district manager. He had watched this unusual man for decades. He had sent him out to one district after another that was a mess, and watched him pull the place together, turn the men around, get them productive and organized: make them into men, a sales force. Now, the man was already a month in the entirely new kind of office he had set up, a first in the country, an office of insurance specialists freed up to help people with estate and pension planning, trusts, and tax shelters. And the manager had opened that new office in January, so while tonight he was being feted for his district's 1963 record, he had already moved on to his new centrally located office on Livingston.

"This man," the VP excitedly took back the mike to say, "is the embodiment of all our great company stands for. He sees our whole society as one, nothing pleases him more than to see us all pulling together, to lift up each and every one of us to the greatest heights.

"He is exemplary. He organizes everyone to do his best, he teaches, he lifts the whole enterprise, he motivates, he inspires. I have known him for thirty years, and it is the greatest pleasure for me to honor him and his whole district here at this event. As I give him this plaque, would the entire field force stand, because the partnership of this leader and his men is what we are celebrating here, and no one could be prouder."

This was the Sert Room at the Waldorf Astoria. It meant Assertiveness, and Certainty, the manager knew, his own, his family's, his district's, his company's. His country's! The man of honor knew nothing of the room's Don Quixote murals, by a stylish rich Spanish muralist named Sert. Who was Don Quixote, after all, but a man whose head was so far in the clouds that he would never buy insurance? The murals showed "The Nuptials of Camacho," but who was Camacho, the rich man in the murals, about to be married to a fair-haired beauty in the richest most tumultuous of celebrations? Who was Basilio, the poor man who, in the nick of time, in front of a thousand celebrants, tricked the rich man out of his bride? And she went with him! She loved him! A battle ensued! Don Quixote with hat and lance and horse, his body thrust forward in the saddle, dashingly defended the poor trickster and his beloved bride. All the honored man knew was that the walls were festive and rich, golden and sepia, with acrobats, singers, and great swaths of drapery celebrating the joy of living, like the event itself. Out of the corner of his eye he had seen his daughter waltzing with spirit with the young man he had found for her. Speak, dance, sell, think, go forward, work.

THE TELEPHONE, 1965

HE WAS USED TO RECEIVING formal letters of congratulations from the top officers at the company. They made a point of sending these letters. It was a style of business that suited him perfectly. It was cordial and old-fashioned, personable and regular. He knew these men from meetings and dinners, from conventions and award ceremonies. Having the support of the official family of officers meant everything to him. The officers knew him like a father knows a son, or a brother a brother. They knew his extraordinary capabilities and record for decades. They were behind him one hundred percent.

"Can you beat that," he said aloud in shock after he read this letter through three times. It looked like all the other letters, the typing was clear and neat, the sentences direct yet engaging, the two paragraphs fit the center of the page with perfect balance, the signature was elegant.

They were terminating him. There was no mistaking the facts of the matter. The letter said he had fulfilled his positions admirably and been an invaluable asset to the company. Now, however, on his upcoming birthday, it was time for him to leave. As he knew well, he would be reaching the age of mandatory retirement, and they thanked him for his years of service.

The call he put through to the officer who wrote the letter threw him. It was as if he reached a machine, a cordial machine. He knew the word for it. It was a cold shoulder. The shoulder was in his face. The shoulder was immovable. The voice was scornful. There were no exceptions or escape hatches due to extraordinary records of achievements and successful initiatives. It was the rule. He must be treated the same as everyone else. And as to the matter of his birth date, it would be out of the question to contest that. The officer said we have no need to see your Turkish birth certificates recently discovered in an attic in New Jersey. For one thing, if they accepted a corrected later birth date for him, it would mean that on his first job, which he had listed on his 1924 application to be employed at the company, on his first job, as a salesman in Rodosto in 1915, he would have been eleven years old. Were they expected to believe he'd held his first job at the age of eleven?

The manager took off his glasses. He put them back on. He straightened some papers on his desk. He called in his office manager. He called in his assistant manager. Everyone knew the rules, but they were in shock. A promotion would protect him and protect his new kind of office, the first of its kind in the whole country. It wasn't a cold shoulder, it was a wall. Something was wrong. He was being stonewalled.

What about A, he thought with slow interest. Go over this dope's head. Selling policies, selling yourself, would you say there is a difference? Day in and day out, taking off his glasses, putting them back on, feeling his way through to someone's need or desire to be charmed and helped, entertained, or relieved of some burden. Relieve the person of a burden, that was it. You have to whirl the question around to the other person's burden. It could take a day or two of strategy, clearing the desk of other pressing matters. Put the facts of the case into order. Think. Pick up the phone.

Mr. A, I'm calling about an important matter I would like to discuss with you at your convenience. It is of a personal nature, and if you would give me ten or fifteen minutes of your time, I would be most grateful. If you'd like, I could come in to meet with you, or we could speak now.

Thanks very much, this is excellent.

I'd like to tell you how proud I am of my district, which last year wound up with the top figure, $317, 000 of Premium Growth. As you know, this continues a career of my many leadership and sales production awards. I've been delighted beyond expectation to be acknowledged by the company in this way, and to get your warm congratulations in person at many of these events.

I was born in Turkey and where I came from during the first world war, boys had to be men at the age of eight or they could not survive. Mr. A, my purpose in speaking with you today is to ask you to correct my age.

Yes, you're aware of course that I've been informed that my retirement will occur next year, based on the date of birth I provided in 1924 when I applied for a position with the company. I would like to give you some background on myself. I gave my age wrong and made myself older when I applied to the company because I was afraid I would not be accepted for the job. Because of my age I had been turned down by another company. I came to this country on June 22 and adopted that date as my birthday.

Mr. A, you know me well, but I think you will find my story about myself and my connection to the company most interesting.

Thank you. First I must tell you how proud we are of our new office. It's the most beautiful office in the country. I was delighted you could join us at the opening of it early last year. The company has always given me the go-ahead, and once again, here we are, with forty insurance specialists, and fifteen agents. It's not a record that you see every day.

Why did I give the wrong age? Well, I wanted to work. I was young, but I wanted to work. You know, today we have too many people who do not want to work.

Thank you, exactly.

I had no authentic records to prove my age. I've only found them recently, my birth certificate. They were among old papers my father left. He and my mother were my dependents and when he died there was no need to look for anything valuable.

In 1940 when this question came up with a letter from the Army, I was under a terrible tension. The company had put me in an agency which was a mess in the Bronx. They put me there because they knew they could count on me to get some order in the district. I was trying to learn my job. We had problems, believe me we had problems.

I know you know. There are many stories in the company which could be written in a book.

Mr. A, I am not just an average representative of our company. I led the country. I am leading the country. The company has recognized my skills and talents. I am now in the prime of my life, enjoying every challenge that comes along. I feel stronger than ever. Did you know I swim three times a week at the YMCA?

Mr. A, why am I telling you what you know perfectly well? You're a gentleman, and you like to have all the facts before you. We built a wonderful office. But my story goes back. As an agent and just off the boat I created three debits where there was one. As an assistant manager in Murray Hill I developed several men to promote to assistant manager when I was promoted. As a manager in Brooklyn I built two districts out of one. I am ready for the best years of my life, the next three and a half years. You watch me.

My birth certificate shows I was born in 1904, not 1901, and therefore I should not retire for three years.

The company asked why I didn't clear up this matter officially when a report was written in 1940. At that time I told the military board my date of birth was 1904, but I didn't ask to change the date officially with the company.

Mr. A, my father's sister left Turkey to settle in France, and in 1940 France was invaded. How fortunate I was to make my future here and not in Europe I cannot begin to tell you.

Mr. A, I am the only one who had the courage to say let's have an office with one hundred insurance specialists. I know that no one else has said that. You've supported me all the way. You gave me twenty-four insurance specialists and I added sixteen more. Mr. A, I feel I can lead any one in the insurance business, and you have backed me all the way, one hundred percent. I have a happy home. Thank God I have four wonderful daughters. You met two of them last year at the Waldorf Astoria.

Mr. A, I've been to the Waldorf Astoria over the years so many times for one honor or another, I feel like it's my living room. The company knows how to honor its men and our wives and families.

Thank you, yes, my wife and I love dancing. And the company throws a good party.

You can't retire me before I turn sixty-five. No one can make me older or younger. This is my age. On my birthday I'll be sixty-two, not sixty-five.

My problem is a simple one. If the retirement age is to be 65, I have my Turkish birth certificate to prove I was born in 1904 not 1901, and the rest is in your hands.

I would like to stay until I am sixty-five, the same as everyone else.

Yes, well as soon as I found my Turkish birth certificate I went to the Turkish consulate to have it properly translated. Although I read some Turkish words, I couldn't do it myself.

Right, 1904. We had to leave the city of Dardanelles with twenty-four hours notice. This was the first world war.

Yes, I was born a week before our holiday of Purim. It's a very festive holiday.

You've heard of it?

You know, all the big men in America were born in February, Washington, Lincoln. I'm delighted to be in their company.

Right, in 1940 when I was questioned by the War Board because although my birth date was listed as 1901 I said I was thirty-six, I didn't make the correction official in the company records because during that time we were all under heavy tension. I couldn't go looking for my birth certificate, and I wouldn't know where to begin. My health was being impaired. To tell you the truth, I felt like taking the next ship and going back to Turkey. I felt I could take care of correcting my age at any time or as soon as I found my original birth certificate.

We were ten in the family, originally, then two died, right, six sisters and brothers.

Mr. A, you've been very kind. I'm sure you have stories to tell about your life also. Your success story could fill a book, and I know you find it a great satisfaction to be a leader in one of our country's greatest companies.

Rodosto, 1915 (II)

THE BOY SAID HE WOULD take the ticket and get his family's bread ration. His parents let him have this responsibility. He put on his jacket and cap to look well dressed. He decided to go to the line first thing in the morning—he wanted to be the first one there. The bakery was a few blocks from where they lived. When he arrived, mobs of people were already there. How could he have made such a mistake? Men and women in huge numbers crowded the street in front of the bakery. Would you call it a line? They spread out in a tense crowd like a big fan. If he waited for his turn, he knew what would happen. By the time he got to the front, the bread would be all gone, and he would get nothing.

The boy stood at the back of the mob. What would you do? Suddenly it hit him. He looked at the people, and they were big. He was a boy. It was not difficult to figure out. This was it. He would get down and crawl through the bottom of the crowd. He would push through the sea of people, and it might not be easy but in minutes he would be in front of the line, ready to present his ticket.

He got on his hands and knees and found an opening. He could ram himself through and ignore anything that anyone had to say to him. After all, he was a boy, and with the ticket clutched in his hand, he knew just what he was doing. He would get to the front before the bakery even opened. He would be one of the first people to get a bread. He pushed and poked his head around legs and persevered with determination. Did other people send their sons to get the bread? No, he was the only one. He saw no other boys pushing their way through the bottom of the crowd. It was only him.

He arrived at the front and stood up. Just as he had wanted, he was right there when the door to the bakery suddenly opened. Inside was a big counter and a big man in an apron. Success was thrilling. He handed the man his ticket and in return got a large bread, the bread of his dreams. But suddenly the crowd came to life, surging to receive what he had under his arm. Now he really had a problem. What could he do? This was the worst thing that could have happened. Everyone in the crowd was surging forward desperate to get their bread, and somehow he had to get out of the way and get home with his crusty fresh-smelling treasure. There was only one way out of the crowd, the same way he'd come in, but now it was much worse. The crowd now was shoving itself forward, everyone with the same terrible fear that the bread would run out before they got to the bakery door.

The boy dropped down to his hands and knees with the bread clutched fiercely under his arm. What happened to him shouldn't happen to a dog. He pushed and shoved and crawled. He fought and rammed himself through. But when he came out on the other end, he was covered with dirt from the street. His jacket was ripped from him. His cap was gone. His knees were cut and covered with dirt and blood. And worst of all, the bread was gone, shoved out from under his arm. Should he go back in and even try to find his cap? It was gone. Everything was gone.

The boy stood up. He had lost the ticket. He had lost the bread. He would go home with nothing. He had nothing to give his family. He had failed miserably. His family would have no bread.

His mother saw him and kissed his streaked face. It's okay, she told him. How could it be okay?

30,000 Feet above the
Atlantic Ocean, 1972

THE MAN'S WIFE AND DAUGHTERS tried but couldn't stop him from working on a loan for a dictator in Africa. They said Idi Amin was a murderer and vicious anti-Semite, and no one, and certainly not a Jew, should lend Idi Amin millions of dollars. The man's family was not just outraged, but angry that he was oblivious to outright personal danger. How could he even think of going to Uganda now?

Gravity had also tried to hold this huge airplane to the ground, but the plane had wheeled itself with quiet confidence along the runway and, after it unobtrusively rolled forward for several minutes, its jets roared, the plane wrenched itself free of the monumental force trying to hold it down, and it was airborne.

The man, forced to retire at age sixty-five from the biggest insurance company in the world, like a captive in front of a firing squad, had won a three-year stay of execution by finding two Turkish birth certificates and explaining why in 1924 (and later) he said he was born in 1901, not 1904. But the three years were up, and in 1969 everyone agreed he was truly sixty-five years of age, the age when retirement was required. How could a man at the peak of his form and the peak of his income, having been such an enterprising effective leader in the field, a many times honored national leader of the sales force, suddenly at the young age of sixty-five be dropped ignominiously from the heights of an impressive income to the depths of a fixed pension? Since he had helped people save and in effect invest their money all their lives, and had worked his way up from selling industrial policies for the poor, to ordinary insurance for the middle-class, and then executive protection policies and other advanced financial packages for the wealthy, he was determined to defy his own demotion to pensioner. His wife had found a front-page article in the *Wall Street Journal*, tore out the headline and lead, and showed it to him with a laugh, "Look at this—this is you!" It was about a man who spent the day on the telephone, had seventy notebooks of phone numbers, and who, amazingly, lived a mile from their house. The newspaper called the man a finder—and gave him a front-page profile because he had already made a million dollars from his deals and mergers. The retired insurance leader discovered a new calling. He was delighted at his wife's only partially tongue-in-cheek goading, and chided himself for wasting so much time on insurance. He became a finder, and because he had friends and relatives on four continents and could get by in English, Spanish, French, Greek, Italian, and Hebrew, his area was international loans.

The finder almost held his breath the whole way the plane ascended, until the Rockaways with their curl of beach shoreline disappeared from view and all he saw was the sky above and the plain blue ocean below. As New York fell away easily and quickly behind them, and the steady pressured engine rush sounds of the jet held their own, his breathing was calm and relieved. He was going to London to negotiate a $10 million loan to a major coffee developer in Uganda; he had two appointments in London, with a Pakistani associate of the Washed Coffee Company and with an officer of an international company based in the Netherlands Antilles which was providing the capital. Why should Amin matter—a hundred countries had authoritarian governments, and Americans were day in and day out furiously protesting their own government and its massacres in Vietnam; besides, everyone knew about the dangerous crime in his own city of New York. Ugandan coffee was superb, with the most pleasing fragrant aroma, waiting to be discovered, and he would launch a development that would help a whole country get on its feet and maybe its dictator—who knows—come to his senses. Of course London was a compromise with the finder's family, and they were all still unhappy but at least he was going. The mild-mannered finder furiously dug in his heels when they tried to stop him, and finally they didn't try any more. The Pakistani associate in London would make the final leg of the journey to close the deal in Kampala. The commission would be split three ways (between the London Pakistani, the finder's associate in New York, and himself). Two years before, the finder had lost a $10 million loan (to Turkey); he had not been aggressive, determined, and available enough; because he didn't pursue it in person, it fell through and the men he worked with had been disappointed and irritated at the expended effort, all the telexes and cables, letters and phone calls overseas, all to no avail. This loan to the Coffee Company the finder was determined to see through.

Married nearly forty years, and never flown by himself before—he had to laugh. He'd commandeered every form of human locomotion in New York, rushing up tenement staircases and subway stairs, grabbing buses, driving and parking his car, walking smartly down and up streets and avenues, riding office building elevators up and down—motion was pleasure, was opportunity, out of the apartment at seven thirty in the morning, off to the subway to do what he loved best, sell, manage, organize, talk, charm, inspire, explain, entertain to focus his men, rally their energies, pull the world together to go forward in prosperity and security, wrangle free of obstacles, hurtle forward with a laugh, help people talk to each other so they could move ahead together and realize what looked like it could not be done *could* be done, people like fellow insurance men, prospects, America, now the world. And he could do this, with no schooling, just charm, determination, an uncanny sense that he was on the right path for himself and for everyone, and would find his way.

"What are you doing," the finder said genially to the ten-year-old colored boy he suddenly took notice of in the seat next to him, who had a notebook open on his tray. It suddenly broke through to him that the boy was traveling alone, and seated on the aisle so the stewardess could easily stop by to talk to him. The boy had a pen in his hand, but had not written a word in the book. The boy had a shy, smart, friendly smile as he turned to notice this white man at his side. The man and boy hadn't considered each other at all before.

"Well, my father told me to write in my notebook once we could use the trays after take-off," he said, obviously inclined to listen to his father. The boy clearly had great respect for his father but no idea where to start. The boy's skin was dark like coffee, a rich burnished brown that the boy must have known was beautiful because of his mother hugging him and telling him so. The man too had been a handsome clever son to his mother.

The man suddenly felt conscience-stricken that he had not offered the boy the window seat so he could see the sky, the ocean, the few clouds. The white man had flown so many times, but always with his wife beside him.

"No, it's okay. I like it here. I just don't know what to write about."

"Ah," said the white man and sat silent for a moment. Finding out that the boy was traveling alone for the first time, and going to see his father, apparently a very famous churchman at a big conference in London, the man learned that the father was always writing—sermons, meditations, a memoir—and the boy was coming to be with his father for a few weeks.

A boy! the world, the future ahead of him. Donkeys and subways, a wife and commissions, awards and children's spouses!

"I could tell you some stories," the finder told the boy.

The boy looked at the white man in the white shirt. The boy's father had not wanted him to watch movies because movies weren't remarkable enough. Maybe this man was remarkable. "Did you ever hear of the country named Turkey?" the man asked. "I'm sure you did," the man said, but then pointed to the boy's bright shirt. "What color would you say your shirt is?"

The boy knew his colors, and didn't hesitate. "Turquoise," the boy said.

"Exactly. Named after the country Turkey—where I was born—because the water all around us was bright as a jewel, blue and beautiful in the sunlight. We used to watch the big ships going up the Straits, with their flags waving."

"Turquoise comes from Turkey," the boy said thoughtfully. The man said as a boy in Turkey he used to like sitting on a stoop eating a juicy head of lettuce, or a piece of melon, or going to school and coming out to play leapfrog, or climbing on the gym he'd made from sticks and rope in his small garden. All his friends used to come by to try it. They couldn't get over it. They paid to play on the gym he built when he was the boy's age.

"You charged them?" the boy said with interest.

"Well, it made it more exciting. They'd come over and ask to climb the ropes and I'd send them home to get a penny and they'd climb on the ropes from one side of the little garden to the other. And then they'd want to get another penny to climb them again.

"I had a lot of friends. We loved to play after school. Just like you do. We'd eat sweets like halvah. We went to school every day. But I'm going to tell you something. One day I was sitting in school with all my friends and suddenly we heard a big explosion that made the whole city shake. Now, you're a smart boy. Think about it. Tell me, what would you do if that was you sitting there in my classroom in Turkey?"

The boy thought. "Everyone had the same question because you all heard it together. The teacher would tell you what to do."

"Exactly, and I bet you know what the teacher said." He looked at the boy. "Run home! Take your things and run home." The finder paused. "They said a ship had exploded in the harbor and when we got home—we could run home in a few minutes—could you run home from your school—no, a school bus—but this was a very small city—a few blocks and we were home, all of us, with our mothers and fathers.

"Now, you know it turned out fine because here I am telling you what happened.

"But that day was frightening. I was exactly your age. It was war and I didn't know what that meant.

"The explosion was a ship blown up in the harbor. What do you suppose happened next?"

"Well," said the boy, "if you were safe where you lived with your mother and father, and the ship wasn't close to you, you were okay."

"That's what we thought. But then the whole town learned this was part of the war. I never really thought about war before. I was just a boy like you.

"We found out we had to evacuate the city. Everyone had to leave. Everyone. The whole city had to be emptied out."

The boy was surprised.

"Because they were afraid the British would drop bombs on the city and they didn't want us to be hurt by bombs.

"Even my old grandmother, who used to sit by the window every day, had to leave? Yes.

"But how would we leave? By ship."

The boy was strong and liked adventure and the man kept the story going. The boy had heard of war but couldn't imagine Manhattan being evacuated. It would be too many people. But this was a small city, the man said, and they left by ship. They crawled up a rope ladder on the side of the ship, one by one, even the very old grandmother, but then the man said he forgot his books and his parents tried to stop him but couldn't. Before you knew it he went down the ship's rope ladder, ran through the streets to his house, grabbed his books, and came back.

The boy looked at the man and tried to picture him as a boy his age dashing through the streets with his books.

"What if the ship left without you? What if they had pulled up the ladder and the ship was moving?"

"The ship was still there." The boy pondered the ways of war and evacuations. The man took a deep breath and paused, letting the boy wait.

The ship out of his city was just the beginning, the man said. It took them to a little town nearby where the whole family stayed for a month, sleeping with two other families on the floor of someone's house. But then they got on another ship, this one a big steamship to take them to safety. This ship was made of steel and was powerful and exciting. But when the families were out on the open water, the man said "something shocking happened." He spoke quietly and looked at the boy. Right next to their ship was a big commotion. "A submarine suddenly came up from under the water."

The boy said he'd been on a submarine in Connecticut once, with his father and mother.

"They were going to blow up the ship we were on. They thought we were soldiers. They thought we were the Turkish army. But we were just families, parents and grandparents and children. What would you do? How would you let them know we weren't the army, not a single soldier on the ship?

"Right. We yelled but they couldn't hear us or didn't believe it.

"Exactly. Very good. All the fathers held the children up in the air. They put them in their arms and held them over their heads. That was in the Sea of Marmara.

"Then what do you think happened? The British said we had to evacuate the ship and go on land nearby.

"Right, they ordered everybody off the ship. Into rowboats, lifeboats, everyone evacuated the ship and headed to the shore—luckily it was close by— and just as we got there, guess what happened?

"Yes. Exactly. That was what happened. They blew up the ship and it sank, right in front of our eyes. No one was hurt.

"And you know what, sometimes you have to evacuate, but it's okay. I've had a happy life.

"People like you and me and your father and mother find a way to have a good life."

The boy asked if he could write the story of the submarine in his notebook for his father—his father would like it. So while the boy wrote about eating lettuce on a stoop and the climbing on the rope gym and up the rope ladder on the ship, and the submarine, and even drew a picture of all the fathers and mothers on the big modern steamship holding their children high up in their arms, the man closed his eyes for a while, pleased and not surprised that he'd given the boy something remarkable to write about in his book. The boy wrote while drinking his coke out of a plastic cup.

Soon the two of them were eating their lunches, tearing off the saran wrap from the bread, using the small fork and spoon that fit so nicely in their hands, buttering the roll. The boy was tearing open the ketchup pack for his hamburger and shoving aside the lettuce and pale tomato; he was hungry and happily accepted the man's pudding, which the man did like but even better he liked the idea of the boy enjoying seconds, and then the stewardess brought the man an extra pudding so they both could enjoy the treat like old friends. Maybe the finder could sell the boy's father a major insurance policy down the line. There wouldn't be time to meet in London, but he'd give the boy his card, and one day, one way or another, maybe he'd look the father up—or back in New York he'd ask his wife to make a Turkish dinner, and the pastor and his wife and son would join them. The finder's daughter would find it so interesting that he befriended a celebrity preacher, a black man, and he did enjoy that; nothing like flying alone to really meet people in the world, although he always met people traveling with his wife, they both liked to talk, trade stories, compare notes, share questions, learn about the world, "get acquainted," he always liked to say.

That's why he and his wife liked Dr. Beck so much. Now there was a smart, friendly, honorable man, intelligent as the day was long, a doctor who had an office in Long Beach, an eye doctor, everyone went to him. The finder could never be educated in the way that Americans were, although of course he'd always read the newspapers, not just the financial pages but the editorials. Still he could never be like people who went to junior high and high school, and college and professional school, and had the leisure to keep up with their education.

But now that he'd been forced to retire, and the doctor invited him to give a talk to their neighborhood garden club on growing cucumbers in your backyard, and they'd become friends and the finder's wife had liked both the doctor and his wife, and the finder's wife suddenly saw that Dr. Beck could pull her husband away from the telephone, she asked him—he was very funny and sophisticated and adventurous—if they'd like to travel, go somewhere really interesting. Dr. Beck popped right back with "How about a safari?" and so that was how they'd gone to Africa for six weeks this past February and March.

The man tried offering the boy the window seat again, and this time the boy took him up on it, peering out the small window at unending sky above them as he steadily and thoughtfully ate his way through every individual animal in the small box of animal crackers the stewardess had brought him as a special treat, eating a lion head-first, a hippopotamus feet-first, a tiger tail-first, turning each animal over in his hand before nibbling it bit by bit or dispatching it whole.

He, the finder, born in Turkey, uneducated, a self-made man: who'd ever thought he'd have two months of travel to Africa with a sophisticated man who knew one African country from another, and who happily took along a sociable likable insurance salesman and his wife. The doctor not only knew one country from the next, but planned the whole trip for the four of them so that for over a month they traveled in a world as different from Turkey as Turkey was from the U.S., confirming all the more how it always paid to talk to people, to be open and interested in everything. Countries that he had never heard of, black people he'd never thought about for an instant, civilizations, lodges, game preserves, waterfalls, the Nile River! the animals.

He thought about that hippopotamus near the hotel, or a giraffe who stood there eating the tops of trees as if this were his world and human beings were nothing. The land and skies were bigger than anything he'd ever seen. Africa, which he had never thought about in Brooklyn, or the Bronx, or Manhattan, had suddenly opened a vast, wild place in his retirement imagination. And the doctor had planned a whole week in Uganda. It was one of the countries Theodore Roosevelt went to after he was President. People had crossed the world to see these animals. There was money in these animals. And so the finder had found equatorial Africa, magnificent in March, high on a plateau, and to think he was traveling it with a medical doctor who knew how to prescribe glasses and perform surgery on the human eye. The finder could have been on the moon, and it would have been no less exciting. In fact there in Uganda they had sat on their veranda overlooking the Mountains of the Moon, in a tea-house hotel. A hippopotamus was standing near the veranda, gazing at them with all of that animal directness that he had known as a boy as he plumbed the depth of his grey donkey's soul by looking into his eyes.

Why was the Ruwenzori tea-hotel in that country more special than anything else on their extraordinary voyage? Why did Uganda seem like the future for the world in some way? Because the mountains of the moon were snow-capped and vast and mystical in the clouds, 16,000 feet high, because they were on a plateau, thousands of feet above sea level, they said, because the country had a new president whom the British and the Israelis both liked, the doctor said, or because the owner of the hotel was Greek, and sat with them like a great host that all great figures of hospitality embodied from Abraham on. Soon they were talking in Greek, soon yes, the hotel proprietor did know the finder's fondly remembered Greek song, "*Samiotisa*" about the beautiful girl left behind in Samos, and another one "*O Polimo*," of course, which bands played at weddings in New York— they called it the *misirlu*. Soon there was talk of what it was like to run a hotel overlooking one of the most beautiful and extraordinary mountain ranges of the world, that was soon to become famous as word got out; soon there was talk of Amin's new government that was boldly seeking development, rejecting the socialism of the man Amin overthrew, thrilling people with his determination.

Business cards were exchanged and the finder over rice pudding, fresh figs, melon, coffee and filo dough crammed with cream was open to the wide world in a way he never could have hope or imagined.

"Would you like a hippopotamus?" the boy injected suddenly into the finder's silent reminiscences.

The finder laughed, his mind crowded with the hippopotamuses and flocks of flamingos, crocodiles and monkeys, giraffes and gazelles he had seen from boat launches and camper vans, from hotel balconies and patios, in vast preserves and along dirt roads through tall grass savannahs and plains. He and the Greek and the Greek's wife and his wife sat on the veranda at the top of the world. They had taken pictures of the four of them with the Ruwenzori Mountains behind them like a moonscape. Selling insurance he had never felt so much on the cusp of the physical world of creation, and at the same time on the edge of the modern, the new and the future. They didn't have any of their pictures. On the way back to Kenya, passing the garnet red and emerald green crater lakes they had stopped at in a preserve, some monkeys chattering in the trees scrambled down and grabbed the finder's bag with all their film in it and it was gone.

When the singing came down to conversation in English, and the Greek learned what the finder did, arranging large international loans for development in various parts of the world, the finder learned that the Greek's brother was currently seeking precisely this kind of capital, for producing one of the hidden treasures of Uganda on the cusp of being developed for export to Europe, America, and Asia.

The boy asked if he played cards. The finder suggested a game of dots instead. A girl across the aisle who had been listening to the stories and had made a big colorful picture of a submarine and the big ship with all the children held up in parents' arms, stood in the aisle and watched for a while. The boy created a large grid of dots on a big piece of paper the man had in his briefcase—it was always better to be ambitious because big games and goals opened everything to big satisfactions. Each of them in turn drew a line connecting two dots, and when the boy connected two dots to complete a box, he got to put his initials in the box, and have an extra turn. The boy said he'd teach the game to his father in London, and he thought his father would find it remarkable.

When they were drinking tomato juice later and pulling salted peanuts out of small foil bags, the finder was recalling in his mind the conversation which had continued in Kampala at a roof-top café. First they'd found themselves talking to two Israeli men. It was the most luxurious hotel in East Africa, and he and his wife had heard Hebrew so began talking to the two men while they were waiting for the Greek's brother. The two men raved about the pay working in construction here for an Israeli company. The pay was almost four times greater than it would have been at home. One of them was getting married the next week, and they all drank and toasted the groom and life.   *L'Chaim!* Then the Israelis left and the Greek's brother came up to join them, on their perch overlooking the seven hills of

Kampala like the seven hills of Rome. There they were once again at the top of the world, the finder taking the initiative to discuss the loan situation in Uganda, and to tell the Greek coffee magnate about his partner connected to funding sources in New York and London. The Greek's partner was a Pakistani with an office in London. "How did you come to work with him?" the finder had asked. "You swam in Dar Es Salaam on the coast?" the coffee magnate said to the finder and his wife. "Yes," said the wife, "the Indian Ocean was hot!" "Well, if you swam straight northeast from the coast, you'd be in India. Indians have been coming here for a thousand years. There are 60,000 Indians in Uganda today. At sunset tomorrow if we take a walk we'll see them, the women in their colorful saris, children running alongside, the smell of spices rich in the marketplace where the families work long days as merchants in the retail trade." The finder's wife was always enthusiastic about a walk.

"You're a brave, smart young man!" the finder said to the boy.

The boy got up to go to the bathroom and then was striding up and down the aisle to run off energy. He zipped by going forward, then back, and again forward and back to ask the stewardess for candy. She found a deck of cards and suggested playing a hand of gin with his friend. So the boy came back and sat down and the man put the deck on the tray and cut it a few times, then was soon telling another story, which the boy wouldn't have thought he was ready for, but something about the man's stories, with submarines and explosions, life boats and ladders, made the boy feel happy. He was probably the only boy in the world who was thinking about submarines in an airplane.

"Now watch this," the man was saying, as if he were in a movie! It was a funny way of talking, but the boy liked it. "There was another evacuation in my family's story. This evacuation was not from Turkey, but from Spain." The man asked, "what would you think if your family and their people had been living somewhere for a thousand years, and were suddenly told they had to leave. They and all their friends and relatives had ninety days to pack up and leave everything behind, everything they owned."

This was a lot for the boy to think about, and he started to bite on the collar of his t-shirt. He liked the submarines and ships.

"The people were crying and praying. Probably if your father were there, he would have said they could stay.

"Sometimes people are mean. Like children saying you can't play on our team, get out of here. Did that ever happen to you?"

"No, I'm a very good player."

"Ah, these were very good players too—in fact the people in Spain worried that these players were better than them."

The boy lifted his eyebrows and started sucking on his collar in earnest.

The man needed a happy ending fast. "Ah, but across a great sea was a country named Turkey. The sultan heard about these fine players. Do you know what a sultan is?"

The boy was right with him. "In that book about the genie in the lamp. There's a sultan, with a big stomach and a big belt."

"Right, a king but he wears a big white turban on his head, and he drinks very strong coffee and sits on a throne."

"Did you ever hear of *Aladdin*?" the boy said.

The man kept going. "The sultan sent ships to greet the people being thrown out, and he said to the people, 'I have plenty of land! Please come live here.' So the people being thrown out were so happy to be welcomed. The port of Spain was filled with ships, one hundred ships with mighty sails, each ship with a thousand people, and that's why my family moved to Turkey five hundred years ago."

The boy suddenly thought of something.

"Isn't London in Britain?" he said. "Well, if the British were blowing up ships when you were in Turkey, why are you going to London today?"

"You're a smart boy. You're really thinking."

He'd skip being thrown out of the insurance company he'd worked at for forty-five years. He'd skip his plan to start life again. He'd skip that his family went crazy about his plan to go to Uganda.

"You see," the white man said, satisfying himself and the boy, "people make mistakes and people change. The British made a big mistake in making Turkey their enemy. They could have saved themselves a lot of problems. They were going to be friends with Turkey. When I was your age everybody in Turkey got together to buy a British ship. It was the most modern and beautiful ship in the world.

We all collected every penny we had—even children. Then at the last moment Britain changed its mind. Britain said they needed the ship themselves. All the Turkish sailors were lined up in a big parade on the shore in England ready for the delivery of that ship. And do you know what Turkish sailors wear? Each one stands very tall." The white man lifted his chest very high in his seat, and as he did, the boy unconsciously lifted his chest too. "And each one wore a round red fez on his head, a special cap like an upside down pail, with a tassel hanging from it on one side. And each sailor wore a long white shirt like for karate that tucked into his big red sash and in the sash was a knife that he kept there. And there were a thousand Turkish sailors on this side and a thousand on the other side, and at the very last moment, what do you think happened?"

"What?" said the boy.

"The British changed their minds and said Turkey couldn't have the ship because they needed it themselves—they weren't going to be on the same team with the Turks in the war."

"So why are you going to London?"

"Later they changed their minds again, and realized the Turkish people were a very fine people, and the Turks forgave them, and we forgave them, and now we're all friends.

"Your father is there now too," he added. "It's a very good country. Didn't your father tell you that?"

"Yes, he said they have the most wonderful zoo, and five hundred people came to hear him talk at Oxford, and we're going to travel around together and have a good time."

"Exactly," said the finder. "Things change and people change, and the world has many opportunities to have good things happen.

"For instance, I had the chance to meet you today, the son of a famous man, known the world over.

"You must be very proud of him. Nothing is better than having such a fine man for your father."

Of course, the finder didn't mention his disappointment that he himself wasn't going to go back to Kampala to be in charge of closing the deal, that he wouldn't return to the seven hills with the Greek's brother sipping the best coffee in the world (he himself never drank coffee, but liked tea or actually a big glass of water to cool off was the best thing), and sit overlooking the city.

The man and the boy put on their seatbelts along with everyone else in the plane. The weather in London was cold. The man was impressed by the boy's questions. The boy liked hearing about the ships and submarines, turbans and fezes, the great Mediterranean and how London changed its mind at the last minute, and then changed its mind again. The boy was excited the plane ride was ending and he would soon be with his father. The stewardess would take the boy by the hand. Did the father look like James Earl Jones, the finder wondered.

PINE STREET, 1988

"IT WAS AN EXPLOSION, crashing noises in my head,"
the man told the contingency case lawyer in his office
on a high floor in a modern building near Maiden
Lane in lower Manhattan. "I was in my hospital bed
when it happened. I began yelling: 'Someone Help
Me!!' I didn't know what was happening. I couldn't
hear and I couldn't see. People came running but
didn't know what to do. I was screaming, 'Help
Me, Help Me!' It happened suddenly at ten in the
morning, and by two it had subsided, but it settled
down to a hiss, like an old radiator valve whistle,
which I've had ever since. It's been a year just about.
The surgery was a full year ago, in January."

The lawyer looked at his shiny shoes, turning his
right foot a little this way and that. His pad lay
blankly on the magnificent table. Strange business
he was in. And would he get back today in time to
see his son's baseball game? His wife wanted him
there.

As if reading his mind, or letting the three of them
take a break to refresh themselves after a stressful
description, the man, who'd been a star in the
insurance business, thoughtfully asked, "Do you
have a family?"

The lawyer laughed. "You're a mind reader! I have
a son and two daughters and one is more beautiful

than the next." He looked over in the direction of the photograph on his desk, but then he smartly recapitulated what they had so far.

"The prostate surgery was in January, with this disturbing incident immediately following it—the morning after. After a month of tests it was established that the urologist had decided on a local anesthesia which was responsible for this explosion, as you call it, causing you to remain even today with a painful and disturbing ongoing symptom which they call tinnitus. The tests could find no other explanation or source of your condition since the surgery. Please tell me the name of the local anesthesia."

The man looked at his notes and said it was two things used in conjunction with one another, and that he had passed out the first time the urologist tried the operation.

"I see you have your hospital records, results from all your subsequent scans, MRI, and analysis of the situation."

The man's wife stood up to look out the window at the streets below. They were on the 36th floor and the city swam like a painting out the window. She was of a mixed mind here. As she'd told her husband, the urologist was the friend of a friend. To go after him would be harder on her husband than on her. But they were both suffering—it was terrible! This was what marriage is, she had discovered, it went on and on. On and on! This time he was always tied up in knots with this constant hissing. Why shouldn't he get some satisfaction and teach the doctor a lesson. Friend, shmend. How could the doctor have not changed the sedative after the first operation when her husband passed out and the doctor had had to stop the whole thing? Then the doctor uses the same thing a couple of weeks later. What on earth was he thinking? This hissing was making a misery of HER life. Here was a lawyer who would take on the case. All right, let's get on with it.

"We'll need to bring in a medical expert on the surgery," the lawyer was saying. "And various doctors will be called to comment on the local anesthesia used." He looked at the paper, and said aloud, as if to clinch the discussion, "Transurethral resection of the prostate."

"What do you think the prospects are?" the man asked, but the word prospect rang a bell in his mind.

He didn't like being on the attack. The pain and suffering were intense, constant, non-stop, but a lawsuit would be painful and stressful to the doctor, a friend of a friend. Taking the man to court was an attack on the man's whole career.

"Hiss, Hiss," went the steam pipe in his head, swelling a bit to fill the room, menacing in its steadiness, the stress of a decision turning up the volume.

The man stepped back from the stress bursting his mind at its seams, and stepped into something more comfortable.

"Tell me about your business," the man said genially to the lawyer, as if to assess the lawyer's competence.

The lawyer said he did several hundred contingency cases a year and he'd been in the business for thirteen years. It had been his father's firm and his father'd had a heart attack and was doing fine, but decided to ease back on the business and give it to his son.

"Oh," said the man, genially and sympathetically.

"Well, you've become an expert on evaluating cases brilliantly to assess the parameters and probabilities."

"Well, that's the business I'm in, and my track record is excellent, as a matter of fact." He gestured as if to say the office's furnishings spoke for themselves of his success.

"Well, you have my entire folder, and I look forward to your assessment of how to proceed." He glanced at his notes to be sure he'd said everything. "I passed out the first time he tried to do the operation, and he stopped. A week later he gave me the same anesthesia, seven and a half mg of valium and 1% of xylocaine together, and when I passed out again, he kept going. This was the most horrible thing. I think the doctor should be taught a lesson on how to select the appropriate anesthesia and I need compensation for what I continue to suffer, which is interfering with my going about my business. It's been a horrible episode in my life and getting a settlement or even going to court will at least give me some redress."

He paused, having pushed himself to complete his peroration.

"So I would like to go ahead with this legal action, and I feel you would be the lawyer to handle the case."

But as the man said this, his mind turned a page, even or especially with the loud hissing spilling into every crevice of his thoughts.

"You're competent and experienced and that, of course, is what I'm seeking."

The man stood up, and shoved the hissing aside. He hardly noticed that he'd just made up his mind to do the opposite of what he was saying, because frankly it wasn't in his nature to alienate people by attacking them. And their friend would be horrified to have his friend brought to court.

The man shifted his weight and his bearing. "It occurs to me that with this law firm, have you considered an executive protection insurance policy? It's my business, you know. I'm sure you have such a policy. I'd be delighted to look over the one you have. It's one of my specialties."

The lawyer was surprised. "Actually, funny you should mention that. I was just talking about that with a colleague. I'm quite interested in looking into one." The lawyer laughed at how this conversation had turned, as if inconspicuously.

"I'll have my company send you an illustration," said the insurance man, as they shook hands. In the elevator, the man told his wife, I just don't want to go through this. I'd rather sell the lawyer a policy.

And he did. The commission was excellent, but left him wanting something more. The urologist had three children also. Insurance was such a pleasure, all positive, all for growth, nothing negative about it. He didn't want to make enemies. His life was about making friends. They always thanked him.

Broadway in Brooklyn, 1982

"So what happened in London in November, 1972, with the loan to Uganda?"

"I arrived in good spirits. I had persevered with my family. The plane was fine. That boy's father was a celebrity. I had a good time. I had a hotel reservation and two appointments. I had my carry-on bag. Everything was in order. I had papers with me for the commission agreement. Rashid Hassan, who had grown up in Uganda, was the Greek's broker in London. He was the point man. He'd return to Uganda and negotiate the deal, once he'd signed the commission agreement—that was always the first step because without it all this work could be for nothing. One third of the commission to Rashid, one third for me, one third for my associate in New York because he knew the lenders, the people with the capital—the funders. It was one of those funders that I had the second appointment with. First Rashid, then Mr. Mills, from the Netherlands Antilles Corporation.

"You see, it's so simple. You have people in business in foreign countries. They want to build or expand or develop their industry. To do that takes capital. Then you have people with money. Well, money shouldn't sit idle, money is the best way to earn money, anyone knows that. So the people who need money need to find the people who have money and want to make it grow. Right. Find. Exactly, that's what I do. Like that man in the market who took my hand and moved it up and down until we agreed on a price and I bought the donkey. Exactly! Okay, the middle man—between the seller and the buyer. Well, that's me, between the lender and the borrower.

"I'm having sardines on white toast, with fresh lemon. You know the funny thing, when we went to Africa on the safari, we spent some time in Morocco and went to a sardine canning factory on the Atlantic Coast and talked to the president. I thought it would be great to be his representative in the United States. They were very good sardines.

"Stick to Uganda? Okay, well I had a very nice visit with Rashid. I went to his house, met his wife, she served me some tea, then she left us alone. I had to apologize to her for all my phone calls, disturbing her at all hours of day and night. She was a lovely gracious lady. And they had a nice flat in London. That's what they call an apartment.

"When she left the room, we settled down to business. Rashid signed the commission agreement. It was no problem. We'd each get a third of the commission. He said he'd go to Uganda. But then he looked me in the eye and asked if I knew about Amin's expulsion edict. Rashid was wearing a good suit, a white shirt, good shoes. His furnishings were excellent. But his face, so familiar to me, so sympathetic, so interested in everything I represented, his olive skin, his dark brown eyes fastened on mine.

"He said, 'We thought it was a joke at first. How could he throw out 75,000 Asians—the shopkeepers and teachers, lawyers and doctors who were running the whole country? How could you throw away the whole economy of a country? It's not possible! We didn't believe it, no one did. Because it didn't make sense. Everything will go into collapse.'

"I had heard something of this, but it hadn't registered with me as a real thing. I was sitting on a dark green couch with a sculpted wooden panel on the top. I put my hand along that carved mahogany to steady myself. 'How is this possible?' I asked.

"'It's not only possible,' Rashid said. 'It's done.'

"I wanted to stand up and yell! This is exactly what a government should not do! Are they crazy? I moved my fingers along the top of the couch, feeling the smooth wood as if running my hand over a beautifully carved piece of wood would restore sanity.

"'Well,' I said, suddenly illuminated with a shocking realization. 'That's what they did to the Jews of Spain. They threw them out. Suddenly in 1492. Well, probably before then, but they gave them ninety days to get out, and they had been the engine of the economy too, and the whole country went into collapse when the Jews left.'

"'But Rashid, how can you go back to arrange the deal?' I asked, suddenly aware of how stupid I had been. I smacked my forehead in shame. 'And how could you not tell me this on the phone?'

"'I'm Muslim,' said Rashid. 'I have connections. Amin is Muslim also. I can do it. I will do it!' he said emphatically.

"'All my friends and relatives there have been ruined. You didn't see the pictures of thousands of my people rushing out, families, hard-working shop-keeping families with their little children? You didn't see it on the television? They've been attacked by Amin's soldiers too.'

"'Then how can you go back?'

"'I'm going back,' Rashid said firmly. 'This commission will save me from bankruptcy. Do you know how hard my fellow Pakistanis, Indians and Bangladeshis too, worked for decades, for generations, in Uganda?

"'If this coffee business grows, it will be money for the farmers, it will be money for my family. This, my dear man, is counterintuitive. But hope is counterintuitive. The coffee growers in Uganda, if they thrive, will dump Amin, they will save the country from this monster. If they starve, he flourishes.'

"'Yes,' I said weakly. What if Rashid were killed when he went back? I had woken terrified from a dream. I was suddenly seeing everything in a new light, although Rashid's counter-intuitions were what had filled my mind, that, and the commission, with glory, all along. If the Greek wanted the money for his Washed Coffee Company and he knew the ropes and the realities on the ground in Uganda, go for it. Do not hesitate or all will be lost. Seize the moment, seize the day, turn the tide.

"My stomach was sinking, nonetheless.

"'And the Jews?' I asked. I looked down at the oriental carpet as I said this. My feet were crossed at the ankles. I reached for one of the biscuits Mrs.

Hassan had set out on the table, as if to instruct myself, matter of factly, that my stomach was fine, and I only needed a British cookie to shore up my resolve.

"'Not good,' Rashid said. 'You know that, don't you? That was before us. He threw out the Israelis, he threw out the Jews. He put goats in the synagogues. He tormented people.' The word tormented hung in the air because he didn't want to say tortured. 'Even Ugandans who had converted to Judaism when they were mad at the British.'

"'The State Department didn't say this,' I said. 'The State Department said this was a rumor. The State Department said Amin was terrible for criticizing the U.S. for our war in Vietnam. And look how many people in the U.S. are also angry about the war in Vietnam,' not knowing what this proved, but just that if you were going to stop doing business every time there was an uproar, you'd never survive.

"'It's hard to sort this out,' I said.

"'Well, it is and it isn't,' Rashid said. 'Let's go ahead and see how far we get.'

"'When I was a boy in Turkey, the government was killing Armenians. Hanging them from trees and gallows. We were all too scared to take them down, so they hung there for a week.

"'But what could you do? You had to keep going, do the best you can. Our landlady in 1915 was Armenian. Her son hid in the basement. He played the oud at night. I used to hear his sweet mournful tunes as I lay next to my mother going to sleep. But what did I do? I went to my mother's cousin to get needles and fabric and I took them to sell because we needed bread. We were starving.'

"'Talk to the backer,' Rashid said, 'then we'll see.'

"I went back to my hotel to put my feet up for fifteen minutes. Then I washed my face and hands and cheered myself on. Then I appeared at Mills's office looking fresh and vigorous, optimistic and ready.

"Mills shook my hand and gestured to a chair in his well-appointed office. It is always a pleasure doing business with successful people. Mills had been contacted by my associate in New York and looked down at the papers on his large polished wooden desk. But in a moment, he was in a rage, in a businesslike way, a British way, with thin lips pressed together, but in a rage.

"'Uganda,' he said sternly, looking at me in shock. 'Your associate never said the loan was to be for a company in Uganda. I have only now received a telex from him to that effect.'

"'To be guaranteed by three banks in Uganda?' I added, as if that were the log to carry us over the creek.

"'My good man,' he began. 'Those three banks are owned by the Uganda government. Their guarantee will mean, you know what? Nothing. Amin is hostile to Western nations. He is nationalizing the businesses in Uganda. Do you know what that means?'

"'I thought,' I said quietly, 'that the British were enthusiastic about Amin because the man he threw out was a socialist, nationalizing everything.'

"'That was at first before they saw what Amin was all about. That was last year! But as of now, the UK has suspended all dealings with Uganda.'

"'I'm sorry,' I said, 'then I'm gravely in error.'

"'Yes, you are,' he said. 'I never would have entertained your associate's interest in this loan.'

"'Will you furnish me with a letter for me to show Internal Revenue so that I can deduct the expenses for this trip? Nothing will be lost to you for doing so, and it will mean that my coming to London will be recognized as a legitimate business expense, which indeed it is. I will be flying home tomorrow; and I apologize for this disturbing misunderstanding.'

"'I will do that right now,' he said gruffly, with a look of embarrassment for my sake on his face.

"So that was the end of that, but I tried to broker many other deals and loans in the next ten years. It was too exciting, too interesting to put it aside. I'm going to give you a list of things I tried to find or arrange for purchase for a commission or a fee, with that same associate in New York or with other people who crossed my path at whatever time, because I liked to talk to people. In that same trip to Africa when I met the Greek Washed Coffee magnate in Kampala, as I said, I met the president of a sardine canning factory in Agadir in Morocco. Your mother-in-law liked that one a lot. 'We could sell your sardines in the U.S., send us samples,' she said. 'Didn't the father of that famous writer Philip Roth try to go into the frozen food business when he retired from selling insurance?' she said.

"But it wasn't just sardines, which as you know, I love. It was things I knew nothing about, like shredded scrap steel bushings, or 2000-ton freighter ships, or 1600 tractors made by Fiat in Italy. Then there were 300,000 barrels of light Sumatran crude oil a day, which Turkey wanted to buy from Indonesia, or a million prime tinplate unlithographed sheets that Saudi Arabia wanted for its Pepsi Cola canning plant. Could we find that? Could we get a good price? Could we broker the deal before someone else did or before a revolution in a particular country meant that buying their oil, like from Iran, was no longer possible? What about bituminous coal for Turkey, or selling a Turk's invention to allow for the transportation of liquid goods in latch-topped containers?

"Mostly it was money, not commodities, we tried for because my associate in New York knew backers with capital to invest.

"Where? In Hungary, Honduras, Brazil, Nigeria, Venezuela, Colombia, Peru, Ecuador, Yugoslavia, Indonesia, Turkey, Saudi Arabia, the Trucial States, they were all needy and desirous, thirsty for capital, grinning and gunning for development, aching for expansion, construction, industry, commerce, trade, prosperity.

"An art gallery in Paris, a shopping center in Panama, a textile manufacturing center in Pakistan, a juice bottling factory and whole cities in Saudi Arabia, a health spa in Mexico, an industrial park in Venezuela, a railroad in Costa Rica, a reconstruction project in China, a hydrocarbon chemical plant in Taiwan, a commercial building in Luxembourg, and mines in Peru.

"Then there were the American opportunities, for a high rise in Chinatown, a 210-unit condominium in Miami, a Deerfield Beach shopping center, an Oklahoma hospital, a commercial bank in New York, an agricultural insurance company in Indiana, and the construction of a major hotel in Atlanta.

"And then the caterpillars. And that's why we are here today.

"All of those wonderful opportunities which I saw and found and organized commission agreements for, all of them for which I scribbled notes, and sent telexes and cables, all of those urgent and very interesting phone calls, and conversations and meetings, all of those cold calls to relatives in far-flung places, which I handled with graciousness and excitement and persistence and conscientious follow-through, came to naught. It was all for nothing. Nothing transpired. Nothing materialized. Not a loan, not a construction site, not a project, not a development.

"Except for the caterpillars. When my long-lost cousin in Peru needed caterpillars, I said, as always, 'yes, I'll get them for you.'

"Then I picked up the phone and called you, my son-in-law.

"'Marty,' I said, 'what's a caterpillar? Those little things in the garden, crawling along?'

"'Very funny,' you said. 'No, it's a construction machine, with huge metal treads on the bottom.'

"'Where do I get them,' I said.

"'Hmm. I don't know. Call the tractor company— Caterpillar— or John Deere.'

"'Okay,' I said.

"And I did and for the first time in my life, I did it right and it was what my cousin needed and I got them to him in time.

"And today we are celebrating that I have received my finder's fee, $2,000. I'm a happy man.

"And I wanted to take you out to lunch to celebrate.

"And to share the finder's fee with you."

"You don't have to do that," his son-in-law said.

"Because now I'm done with being a finder. It's over. I've found—myself, as the young people say."

The bill at the luncheonette was $6.79 for his sardine sandwich and his son-in-law's grilled cheese.

He left the waitress a $10 tip and they left the Brooklyn coffee shop where he'd gone to take his good-humored son-in-law to lunch to celebrate his retirement from being a finder, twelve years after he started.

"You know," he said, "I enjoyed every minute of it. Nothing is better than sitting down and talking to people. Everyone wants the same thing, to get ahead. All over the world."

Broadway in Manhattan, 1997

"Another birthday card? How many daughters do you have?" asked Raj, sitting on his throne, a high office chair at the cash register in his small packed kingdom of paper supplies. He could have been wearing a turban in a nineteenth-century painting, sitting cross-legged, instead of in a small shop on Broadway, in a white button down shirt, his stomach confidently bulging over his belt.

"You have so many questions. What if I asked you some," the shopper, who was in his nineties, asked, and laughed as he looked quietly through the standing carousel for a card with big flowers and swirling script conveying exactly what he always wanted to say, "You are beautiful I love you my daughter many happy returns of the day." The old man, trim, spry, upright, always chose quickly, then reached in his pocket to pay.

"So how many daughters do *you* have," the shopper asked the store-owner with a smile.

"You're so nosy, aren't you?" Raj laughed as he put the card in a slim paper bag meant for cards.

"Well, I see you've opened three stores on Broadway now. You're an excellent businessman. You know what you're doing. Because to do well you must set your sights high, be ambitious, spread your wings, don't hold back." Then, musing on the shop-owner's success, he added, "Three stores, you have many employees."

"Ugh, you're such a talker." Raj held back from handing him the card in the slimmest of bags. "But it takes one to know one. I'm curious what your business is. You're still in business now, always in a hurry. You're doing something, I know that."

"Raj, I'm surprised at you, so smart and you don't know what my business is."

"Anyway how many daughters do you have?" Raj went back to that. "I have two daughters and one son. They're all very smart. They're all in college."

"Raj, we live in a fast world. In the old country we would have sat down, had some coffee. Played some backgammon. What do they say, chewed the fat."

The man was so slim, Raj admired the contrast with himself. But Raj also admired his own belly, his own smile, his business acumen. "So what country are you from, my friend?"

"I'm from Turkey. And you're from Bombay. I know. Your friend over there, your sales clerk told me. Nice young man, from the Dominican Republic. A young man but with a wife and children already." Then he added, "Bombay, there's a big city. A world-class city. But you came here. Very smart."

"Yes, but I sit in my store all day getting fat, while you're always up and running."

"No, you look in excellent health. Robust, with a sense of humor. A good family man. I met your wife once."

"Ugh, she's always angry at me," Raj joked, making a face and laughing.

"Because you work too much," the spry man said. "My wife right now is standing in the kitchen saying *what is taking him so long. He only went to buy a card. We're supposed to leave to have a birthday lunch with our daughter and son-in-law.* She says *it's a Sunday, we have a date, he's probably selling insurance.*"

"Ah," said Raj, finally having his answer. "You sell insurance, what kind of insurance?"

"Come on, with your three stores, you have all the insurance you need. You're a very clever man. Liabiity, Raj, Executive Protection, Disability for your workers. Health insurance for your family. Theft. I'm sure you have it all."

"You know," said Raj. "I need a new disability policy for my employees."

"Now look," said the trim wiry man. "Are you trying to get me into trouble with my wife?"

"What company do you work for?"

"Raj, if you need insurance, I'll get you whatever you need. Let me look at the old policy you have and I'll bring you some illustrations tomorrow."

By then the Dominican sales clerk was standing at his side. *Mi esposa*, he began with a respectful Spanish comment about his wife wanting him to get life insurance, because he smokes and it makes her crazy.

"Ah," said the shopper, "if you give it up for a year, I can sell you a non-smoker policy, which will save you a lot of money. But look, I better go now. My wife is having a fit. I know where to find you tomorrow. And we'll sit down and take care of everything. Mr. Rodriguez, don't worry, you're going to stop smoking. You have three children, your family needs you, no wonder your wife is worrying. Do you need a doctor to help you quit?"

Mr. Rodriguez thought about that. He had a sweet polite face. His hair was neatly combed back. He never did things quickly. His children were all in parochial school. Everything was expensive. This was a second job. His wife wanted him to go to church on Sundays. Stop smoking? Just like that? He smoked to worry and to forget to worry. But if he stopped he could save money on his insurance. His wife would be thrilled.

"Tomorrow," the card-shopper said to the two prospects.

"By the way," he added, "why did you ask me what country I'm from?"

Raj said, "because I like you. You're from the old country. You're serious. You're funny. You're not from Bombay but you're from the old country."

The shopper asked the young man in Spanish what his boss's language is.

"Hindi."

"And maybe Raj, you'll teach me some Hindi too. If we're going to do business together, I want to learn something new. I don't know a word of Hindi."

"Oh, get out of here. I bet you speak it fluently."

The old man left, pleased with his purchase and prospects, and looking forward to seeing his daughter.

It was many years now that all his daughters were married, but it still gave him pride and relief that allowed him to breathe and celebrate. He no longer had to have panic attacks and touch the little valium pill he kept in his suit jacket pocket, that having survived the Inquisition and the Nazis, starvation and the wolves of Inecik, it would all stop there, in his line, with unmarried daughters, with nothing to show for all his determination and passionate desire to survive.

Boardwalk along the
Atlantic Ocean, 1958

HE WAS RUNNING and he had several songs running in his head.

He breathed in the air with its salt edges and seaweed smell. He felt the newly risen sun on the bright people-less shore, the ocean meeting the sky at the horizon. He was alone at 6am with the gulls screaming as they veered in wildly turning arcs and dips to the jetty and up the sand. The ocean rolled in and out with the slow shushing sound of steady breathing, sliding up the sand and pulling back in a series of thoughtful and thoughtless offerings and retractions.

As he ran, the narrow planks of the boardwalk quietly jostled in that gentle honkey tonk of old boardwalks.

Exalted and hallowed be God's great name in this world of His creation. Amen.

He could run because he could breathe because his mother was no longer in agony and he was no longer in an agony of guilt that he had not found a way to lessen her agony. She screamed in frustration and anger when he last saw her in the hospital; this was not the mother he'd known, his business partner in childhood adventures of survival when the food was gone in the War. "You eat," she used to say. "I've already eaten."

Honkey tonk.

May His will be fulfilled by the revelation of His sovereignty and the flowering of His salvation. Amen.

How many times would the circle go around in his head? He was the provider, the businessman, the manager, the salesman. Would she have wanted him to drop everything to take her into his house, to demand his wife take her in and shelter her when his sister said it was time for her to go to the Home but the Home could not take her and instead she went to the hospital.

No! She wouldn't have wanted him to come to a dead halt, and go back to a standstill of no money. Nothing! She wouldn't have allowed that. He had his children, and his business; she would have said, no, don't do it. You are my business partner. Keep going forward. Don't get pulled back for me. He knew his mother. His mother had always counted on his going forward. Keep going, she'd say. She'd laugh.

He watched his sneakers on the boardwalk. His feet pointed forward without confusion, his body was tall, his arms keeping his body company: keep going.

But was that it, that she should have been there for him, to send him and his into the world, to go further and further, to break free of the pulling back into nothingness, that she should have propelled him— and oh that laugh—"she used to laugh!" he'd say, and his father would look in the doorway with that quizzical look on his face—what was she laughing at? who was she laughing at—"she used to laugh" and that laugh had always made the man running now along the boardwalk at 6am happy, because it meant she was proud of him for moving ahead, for being a child man, and then a grown man, for breaking away from whatever was holding him down in the old country, for centuries, because there was nothing that a man could do there to make money, and it was the end. But was that it, that she should have been there to propel him, but he didn't need to be there for her?

May He hasten the coming of His anointed Messiah in your lifetime and in the life of the whole house of Israel, speedily and soon; and say ye, Amen.

He got to the metal bar at the end of the boardwalk and touched it and turned.

Although the breezes from the ocean washed both the anxiety and relief from him, he was sweating in the early morning August sun.

At home he'd shower and dress for business and make himself rye toast and olive oil, a cup of yogurt with a cut-up peach, some juice.

Then the best tide of all, at seven he'd walk crisply out the door to join the men, be recognized, greeted, welcomed, quieted at the synagogue a block from his house. It was what he needed, a group of men, who looked like him, who made a living, the providers in the homes all around them, in the white shirts, the ties, the humor, the understanding of the perils and dares of a man's life.

He was there every morning at seven. They knew his name. He got to know theirs. Each one was a

story of work and women and children and a Jewish
father and a Jewish mother.

Honkey tonk.

Be His great name blessed forever, yea, throughout
eternity.

His breathing sounded his exertion. He was in his
prime, and a strong thin man. But he was sweating
as he pushed. How did others do it, he wondered,
without running every day in the morning, how
did they lose their most wonderful mothers without
saying Kaddish every day, how did they joke with
their wives at dinner without having that early
morning daily brotherhood?

"She always laughed," he said, feeling his sweat
pouring down from his scalp saving him from
having to decide between grief and relief, fear and
pleasure. "Keep going" is what she wanted.

Kaddish was nearly a thousand years old. His
father had said Kaddish for *his* mother and *his* father.
Kaddish felt as old as the gulls spinning in wild arcs
around the glory of the sun-spangled ocean.

But running was new.

He would find that book and buy copies for
everyone he knew. The first guide to jogging, the first
guide to running. And for the rest of his life every
morning he would jog, on the boardwalk, on the city
streets, on his living room floor in his socks when he
was ninety-eight years old.

The men in the minyan were there for him every
day, just to be there with him and each other, to pray.

Not to sell insurance, not to manage an office of
agents, not to inspire, not to provide.

And yet in the small room in the shul basement, with its plain walls and odd assortment of plush and rickety furniture, as he got to know them, well, of course, one day they would say, as they were heading out the door, "I understand you sell insurance."

His mother used to laugh, when they were starving, and when she was cooking great feasts.

The name of the most Holy One be blessed, praised and honored, extolled and glorified, adored and supremely exalted, beyond the power of all blessings, hymns, praises, and consolations of this world to express; and say ye, Amen.

* * * * * *

Manhattan, Dinner at Eight, 1953

The small apartment was silently simmering, like dinner on the stove. The woman was waiting for her husband, the successful insurance man who, as usual, was infuriatingly late coming home from work. The opened table, filling almost the entire foyer, had been set with simmering resentment by the oldest daughter. The two younger girls meanwhile had been playing with a Ginny doll, for which the middle daughter had made a wedding dress beaded with a tiny string of pearls along the waist and the top of the hem of the white taffeta skirt, and with two pearl-beaded straps holding up the taffeta bodice, showing the little doll's bare shoulders, and hinting at its tiny innocent breast buds beneath the fabric.

The door slipped closed behind the husband with the sound of finality that only a solid rent-controlled Manhattan apartment front door can make, at once heavy and light, clanking like a gate in the old country. The wife's anger boiled up like the furor of potato water on a high flame, hissing into a steam explosion of sputtering. She considered but overruled calming herself as if by shutting the burner. They could sit down and eat, at least, and the next chapter of the day could begin, so they could get onto the next and the next, for what she didn't know.

The husband slipped in sideways between the table and the wall, and handed his wife the late *New York World Telegram and Sun* where she would check the closing stock prices. At least he had the paper—the other night he'd forgotten it and she'd lashed out at him, as if she'd been a prisoner in confinement locked in by domestic love and prerogatives to make magnificent Sephardic vegetables with Italian parsley and tomatoes and salt.

As he came around the square of the table, he also took off his hat and coat and scarf and gloves to put them in the foyer closet.

"You're very late," she announced from the small kitchen in a firm voice. She'd already checked the closing stock prices and was cheerfully vindicated in the choice of stocks she'd decided to buy the previous week. She was smart, she knew it, she was clever, and had business sense, and it all meant that her aspirations to be a brilliant modern woman of the future were, as always, suffocated in confinement to her round of tasks, nurturing girls who resented her dictates and bossing, and rebelled against her at every moment they could, at least the older one, and in sneaky little ways the middle one also.

"Let's sit down," the husband said standing at the richly laden table, a grand wooden bowl of salad and a china platter of zucchini-rice-tomato-parsley joy spread out gorgeously before him. He saw the thin steak on a bare dish looking him in the eye and bristled as if he himself were the fat that was cozily strung along the edges. He wouldn't say anything about the steak which she knew he hated. He would ignore it, after all he was hungry, and knew to contain himself and be a good father who loved his wife and three daughters.

He took up his glass of red wine and sang the blessings as if the very words themselves were the greatest gifts from God, which they were. *Baruch Ata Adonai, Elohenu Melech Haolam*. Ah, it was his life, his hope, his desire, and the singing that let him breathe. However, she said, *"I* made dinner" as if to say, she, not God. That made him take a piece of the steak onto his plate as if to push her provocation to its climax, but really he was hungry and needed to eat a real meal, and she often made the fish he loved, serving it up with the oil and lemon sauce from the platter, so why not think positively, and he could ladle himself the comfort of the *calabaza* (the zucchini) and indulge himself on perfect faith and pleasure in the sauce of the tomatoes and parsley and rice.

But she was after him, so when he happily asked about their day, and heard they went ice-skating at Wollman rink in the afternoon, and it was sunny and cold at the rink with the three girls, each dressed for skating and with white boot skates that fit each one the way they should, laced up perfectly, and she, his wife, also in her skates out on the ice, he was proud of his family, proud of his wife for her exuberance. At the same time, however, he was worried, his stomach dropping way down as if to his feet as he put down his fork, and sat there calmly waiting for the calamity. Then she said it, just as he expected.

"And Dr. Wissenkraft was teaching Miriam the 'sow cow'."

The husband said nothing.

"He's so patient, and such an excellent skater, and he spent a full hour. She's making excellent progress and loves the attention, you know."

"He's a doctor. I don't understand what kind of doctor only works in the morning and has the rest of the day off. He only works three hours a day. Then he's there every afternoon, with no wife and no responsibilities. What kind of man is that?"

He paused, then added firmly and slowly as if he'd figured it out to his satisfaction. "He's not really a man if he has nothing better to do than to skate with another man's children every afternoon."

This was too good to ignore. While her husband calmly picked up his fork and knife to cut himself another bit of steak, and put it in his mouth, Miriam, the oldest daughter, thought to jump in while the two younger children felt the electricity in the air and kept their faces to their plates as if they were feeding the Ginny doll, not themselves.

"I'm very happy to be learning the 'sow-cow.' My figure skating teacher, Mr. von Eisner, sticks to the figures, and I must do them perfectly, it's like mathematics. This is different and exciting. Besides, Mr. von Eisner keeps a pipe clenched in his teeth while he skates, and he's grim. Dr. Wissenkraft is teaching me jumps and ice-dancing too and we dance together."

Miriam was no innocent in this. She knew the game, that these perfectly true remarks would scratch the surface of calm off her father's warmth. Then he would explode at his wife, and Miriam would have the satisfaction of getting her mother yelled at; after all, Miriam had been forced to set the table while the two younger sisters were busy playing. Not that Miriam thought this through consciously but putting in her two cents provided the anticipated pleasure of vengeance for her mother's bossiness. Anyway, ice dancing in a man's arms was not to be criticized, and she was defending her mother at the same time.

The father meanwhile could not chew the steak. He put down his fork. "You know I cannot chew this meat and yet you make it anyway." He paused. "I'm sure you gave me this on purpose."

"Your beloved mother spoiled you in Turkey, don't you know that?" She paused and took a deep breath, balancing her own desire to unleash her pent-up spite against the desire to see her three daughters enjoy the steak, the zucchini, the frozen American peas that she served to feel like an American for a change, and because the color reminded her of summer and bright sun on the grass behind the small house where she grew up in Pelham Bay.

The wife's jab number one about his mother: "She had no teeth, so she never made meat and you never learned to chew."

Next jab: "She spoiled you rotten, catering to your every wish as if you were God's gift to the Jews."

Jab three: "And just because you went through starvation during the First World War doesn't mean I have to cater to your every whim. The children can have steak if I want, this is America, and if you don't want it, don't eat it."

He tried to eat it, but his dentures rebelled, those usually well-behaved and friendly fixtures in his mouth. He'd lost his teeth too many years before, there was a price to be paid for early hardship, even hardship that had been brilliantly overcome, he and his mother together, with long treks deep into the countryside to barter fabric and needles for eggs and wheat. It was hard to decide whether the insult to his manhood was more or less of a hardship than the dryness of the small square of meat in his mouth that he could not chew or swallow and which his innate politeness would not allow him to spit out.

"And as for spite," his wife struck again, "you go to work every day and yet you refuse to let me get a job." She knew she was well within her rights as a woman to say what was on her mind. She knew what women could do, Rosie the Riveter and a million movie stars in their furs and gowns, like in *Dinner at Eight*, that movie she'd never forget because it proved, if you paid attention, that women knew best. You think they're feeble and ridiculous, but in the end it was clear Women Knew Best! Besides, it was good for her three daughters to see she wasn't a timid female, kowtowing and catering to a man's rules.

He took his paper napkin to his mouth and brought the small piece of meat neatly wrapped down to his plate. He forgot everything, he forgot the men in his office who treated him with camaraderie and respect, and the girls, all those clerks, dressed in puffy dresses, who had the utmost respect for him and his warmth, and enjoyed every minute of their days at the office with clearly set tasks in good company and the paycheck at the end of each week that gave these unmarried girls pride and a feeling of accomplishment.

He forgot that he had let his wife prevail upon him to move the family from the Bronx to Manhattan. They had left the Bronx which was packed with Jews—Bronx Park East—Turkish Jews and Russian Jews, whole families immersed in a crowded Jewish world where they jostled from butcher to school to dinner to Shabbat to synagogue to greetings to cooking to children playing in the park. She had said Manhattan would be better for the children, a better school, closer to his job, but here they were, he thought, in a Jewish desert with no *real* Jews around (except for the printer upstairs who was touched when he was needed for a minyan), no synagogues, just intellectuals and artists and he didn't know what, while he himself had only gone to school until he was ten. Husband and wife were fish out of water flopping on the boat, flapping in nowhere-land. Where were they going, why hadn't they stayed with the Jewish neighborhood; she was so terribly clever but he forgot all of that and began to look ahead and beyond his daughter Miriam to the wall.

Dr. Wissenkraft! He had terrible nerve. Taking my family sailing in the summer while I was working hard to support them. Then in the winter, these daily ice-skating lessons. The husband panicked. How was he going to handle this? The pain built up in his chest.

Usually when things got tense at the dinner table, he got up in a dignified way and simply left the table, striding into the living room behind him, or pretending to stride—he was really running away. He'd put his feet up on the coffee table and maintain a strict silence and ride the storm out.

But today, he found he was not running. The three girls were seated like dolls around the square table overfilling the foyer. It was important to show them something, and he felt in a new drastic mood.

"I don't want my family seeing Dr. Wissenkraft any more," he said clearly and firmly, the skating man looming peevishly in his mind, that Dr. Magoo face, those ruddy cheeks, the bald pate, always smiling, what did this Dr. Wissenkraft want? It was such a relief usually to beat a retreat. In the living room, the bathroom and, if need be, the three girls' bedroom, he could hide. That was it, those were the spaces available to him when he stood up and ran from the table. He could go to the end of the living room and look out the window down on 12th Street, past the gauzy curtains by the baby grand piano, and maybe breathe. Although beating a retreat didn't look good, it was for preserving family peace, not inflicting the terrible unacceptable conflict on his daughters, not yelling, not exploding, rather preserving his dignity, even if it seemed cowardly.

But what had he just said? The space of the apartment was small, and when he left the table he really wanted to clear a space in his head, that's what he wanted. Usually he could not do that. But he had heard himself speak calmly and with a firm resolve. Look at that! And he wasn't budging. He was the father of the family, the breadwinner, the provider, everything on the table was possible because of him.

He repeated his statement, so uncharacteristic of him in the first place but now as steady as the muscles in every part of his body. He was firm, he was fit, and it had come straight out as if hopelessness were turned aside with an easy gesture, as if he were putting down a piece of paper he didn't need or want. His whole repertoire of charm and sweetness and humor and resilience that was his brilliant low-key resource every minute at work was not relevant at this moment.

In that pause of calm surprise, of course, his handsome wife was staring at him in disbelief. She'd never heard anything like this from him. His bit was to get up and run from the insult of her disrespect. He'd say, "My mother would never dream of talking to my father that way." She'd say, "Who cares? This is 1953, not the Middle Ages in Turkey."

"What are you talking about?" she slammed him with, rising to the pleasure of a good fight, of fury at his violating her rights.

He stood up but kept his ground.

"I will not have this man interfering with our life. I will not put up with this."

"But you are always working!" his wife exploded. "If he is willing to go ice-skating with us when you're at work, I'll be dead before I allow you to take that away from us."

The middle child stood up at her place, sensing danger, pushed her chair in and stood up in the six inches between the wall and the back of her chair. She was helping her little sister get up too, and both of them had their plates in their hands, while a switch of rage in the man had suddenly switched on, the only moment in his whole life when humor and charm decamped.

"I will not have it, do you understand?" he said.

Sticking to his point was effective in producing shock, but he knew his resolve needed punctuation to complete its effect. He felt he was out on some outcropping, his arms flailing in the wind, the land around him wildly static, the sea crashing against the pilings of the pier, it wasn't a movie, it was Turkey, the Sea of Marmara. He picked up his wineglass, turned quickly to the wall, and overcoming thousands of years of inherited calm and sweet schooling in family harmony, hurled it at the wall just two feet away from him.

It crashed.

The family always said *Kapara* when a glass broke. It meant "It's O.K., don't be alarmed." It was comforting, as if that glass were for God. It's Hebrew, not Turkish. But this was different. No one said *Kapara*. The mother had squeezed around the side of the table, to usher the three girls into the small back bathroom where a two-foot plastic Christmas tree lived in a cardboard box from year to year in the unused shower-stall. The bright green American peas rolled gently and knowingly on their plates as the girls settled down on the closed toilet seat and the floor to eat dinner away from the danger of crashing glass. And no one saw Dr. Wissenkraft ever again, that ruddy fifty-year-old bachelor, or if Miriam practiced the waltz jump and learned the sow-cow with him, she did so when no one from the family was there.

They soon gave up on Greenwich Village and moved to a modest house with a synagogue around the corner. It was the wife's idea. The psalm said a woman of valor "sets her mind on an estate" and "acquires it." The wife hired a decorator for the house, and she liked going to Tuesday afternoon Bible Class with the other women in the neighborhood led by the synagogue's rabbi who discussed all sorts of things with them about Joseph, Job, Sarah, and Rebecca, and in a very eloquent manner and with utmost respect.

And as in Manhattan, they went dancing every Friday night, and on Saturday mornings when her husband was at synagogue, the wife sent the middle daughter to a Singer Sewing Machine Store sewing class where three squat short-waisted bulbous women helped her (the only student) make a dark grey-black scratchy wool jumper with crinkled polka dots like peas from a can a hundred years old. At least it was a really long walk to the sewing shop, however, and the daughter had it all to herself and would spend an hour at a Five and Dime looking around at all the wonderful little things one could buy if one wanted anything—but she didn't. The walking part was best and, of course, she'd never wear that horrible black jumper. Every night her mother played the baby grand piano at midnight and her mother's happiness soothed her to sleep, and she knew that both her parents loved her.

The Kitchen in New Jersey, 1958

Where were the grocery stores with plywood
sidewalk bins of onions and oranges? Where could
she buy flat parsley? Where was 170th Street, and its
little newspaper and barber shops? Where would she
be if she walked out the door? Where could she walk?
Where was the dusty park near the courthouse? She
peered out the window. No one was walking down
the street. There was no one to talk to out there.
Where was she?

She was in a big house on a street with trees. The
house was like a vast impediment, to what?—to her
thinking by walking herself on her errands. Rooms
and rooms of the house meant nothing to her. She
could go up the carpeted stairs and stand on the
landing. But what for?

Downstairs again if she opened the front door—
"Mom, where are you going?" her daughter would
call out—she would stand on the doorstep and look
at all the other impediments, white painted houses,
with not even a car in sight, and no people at all, just
tulips in a circle and green grass pasted on here and
across the street.

Real houses were dark red brick, they stood together,
right up against each other, packed with families in
apartments—you could call out the window to the
children downstairs to come home for supper, or

the buzzer would ring, the elevator would slide up hesitantly and creakily, slow and dependable while the person in it collected her thoughts. Apartments had windows looking out on the grey cement wall of the alley, and your singing while cooking in a tight little kitchen was a great joke and a great joy.

Where was she? What was she looking at on these endless streets, as if with no one there and nowhere to go? Just trees, low squat houses, a sky that took over like a big umbrella that didn't know or care that she was there. Could she talk to the sky? She never had.

In America she'd lived on Lexington Avenue in a tenement packed with families, then on Westminster Road on a short gritty block near the Prospect Park Parade Grounds in a red brick apartment house, and then, when the children were gone far away, on the Grand Concourse on the third floor, one of those buildings with a narrow paved entrance that sucked deep into the center of the building so the apartments on either side could have some light.

A linen closet. That was something she understood. It wasn't as good as walking to 170th Street to buy parsley and onions for the matzoh meat, which she couldn't do here, but her daughter said it wasn't Passover yet anyway. But she could, she decided with determination, clean out the linen closet. She'd find it. Every place she'd lived in since Turkey, they had a chest or closet with sheets, *sabanas*, and a few tablecloths. You could stand in front of it admiring the bundles and folds of white. Here they had a whole closet, which she knew because she'd seen it. You could take a deep breath, then another deep breath, and then just take everything out shelf by shelf by shelf, and once everything was out all around you, you could decide what to do next. She reached up to the top and that was good stretching, and she liked bending low also to put everything down on the floor, and using her arms and body in this important purposeful dance of women's work.

"Mom, are you okay? What are you doing? I'll be right up," her daughter called from downstairs.

Then the daughter showed up. "Oh, Mom, what are you doing?"

The little mother, stooped and shrunk now, stood in the center of a pile of blankets and pillows, aprons and tablecloths, pillowcases and bedspreads, washcloths and embroidered cushion covers. "Don't hit me," she said to her daughter, fixing on her daughter's face distraught at the mess.

"Mom, why would I hit you?" the daughter said, even more distraught at the horror of such a thing. Why had her mother said that? What a shocking terrible thought. Everything in Turkey where the daughter grew up had been so hard, with the War and no food, and terrible long walks in the countryside and their father gone for years, and no money and the long frightening ride across the Atlantic. Now finally this was good in the beautiful suburb of South Orange, the daughter thought, with her husband and two sons, not that they were easy, but with these trees and beautiful houses, she could breathe. It had been a haul getting here, with her husband's time in dental school, and the service, and living in the South in a tiny crammed apartment while he was there. Now they were in paradise, American paradise, the best, in a beautiful New Jersey suburb. But what would she do with her mother? She'd had to transplant her mother from that cramped little apartment on the Grand Concourse; she couldn't stay there any longer, but what was the plan? Her mother had shrunk down so much it was hard to remember that crabby bustling laughing singing tall lady that had bossed her through the War. It was hard for the daughter to remember anything but that dog that bit her on the inside of her leg, and hunger, and eating crusts dipped in vinegar in a rusty can.

But now they were free. True, her sons were not easy, and her husband took a belt to them, was that right? He had that old-fashioned way from when he grew up in the tough neighborhoods of Atlanta. Yes, he was Jewish but he grew up in America. How would she hold it all together, two sons, a husband, his work downstairs in his dental office, the food, the cooking, getting the boys to grow up right, do their homework. "You want to smoke," her husband had said to his ten-year-old sons. "Sit here, you'll smoke a cigarette and get it right." And they'd coughed like crazy and he made them smoke a whole cigarette each until they were blue in the face.

But the house and the street gave her a feeling of hope, as she looked out the prettily curtained windows in the kitchen. Of course she made the curtains herself. This was what it meant to have a future, to live on a street like this, in a white house with an upstairs and downstairs and a train set arranged on a big old table in the basement. They were Americans, and that was what you wanted, trees and grass out the front door, not old people and poor people, not elevated trains, not subways and dirty little stores, but sky out the front door, so when her boys took out the garbage at night they could look up and see the stars in the sky.

Passover was coming and that was good. The eighty-five-year-old lost woman could work, the way she used to, singing, proud, purposeful, her body knowing who she was. Her daughter had bought all the ingredients. They had created the shopping list together, although this, the mother felt, was very stupid. What would you want a list for? You were cooking, you knew what you needed. In Turkey in the little house, her husband would run to the market and buy just what she needed. In America, proud new land, she would run to 170th Street and return with her sack of just what she needed, and she'd meet friends on the way there and back, and chat in the streets with them, *Ke haber?* How're you doing?

But at least her daughter wouldn't yell panicked and angry to her, "Mom, what are you doing?" or if she did, claiming her voice was low and gentle, the answer was not a problem. I'm making matzoh meat, *mina de karne*. She didn't have to worry that the woman of the house would hit her.

"Mom, why on earth would you think I would hit you? I would never hit you, you are my mother, Mom, did you ever hear of a daughter hitting her mother?"   Maybe because now she, the daughter, was the tall one, and her once tall mother was little? She'd been so good to move her mother into the house, close out that small cramped apartment in the Bronx; she'd taken care of all the furniture, and boxed up all the dishes and pots, and Turkish pots, and thrown out that flat enamel pot with handles and round depressions for making *bimuelos* or leek patties—*keftes de prasa*. "Where are my pots," her mother had yelled in panic. Well, especially with this level of panic bursting from her every day, they could not let her stay alone in the Bronx, maybe they could not even let her stay here.

The doctor said her mother had agitation probably because her starvation during the first world war in Turkey was not good for the brain. There was famine, wasn't there, he had asked. He had talked to the eighty-five-year-old woman in Ladino, sympathetically, and gently, but the shrunken woman was worried. She no longer was the tall and solid joking and singing woman she'd been since marrying in Canakkale. Instead she was quiet, solemn. And then of course, her husband had died years before because he was too stubborn to take his heart medication, but she'd been fine for years living on her own.

Mina de karne had allowed them both a pause, a reminder of the things that were right and orderly. Her daughter used to bring her husband and two little sons, and her son would bring his wife and daughters up to her seders on the Grand Concourse, and cooking and preparing for them had been all she wanted. Her husband, of course, used to do the seder in Hebrew and Ladino, and they sang songs into the night in the tiny living room made into a dining room with opened bridge tables.

But now, what was left? The mother would make *mina de karne*, with the knife cut three large Spanish onions into a great pile of little pieces, and brown them in olive oil. She stood over the stove turning the soft onion pieces tenderly, her curved back making her into an intent bird by the stove, with so many onions she had to take some out and put them into a soup bowl to go into the refrigerator for something else.

The sweet oily smell of them entered her mind, as did the wooden spoon quietly with just a tap tap to stir the pot; it was soundless, reminding her of a phrase from a song, so it stumbled out of her mouth without her hearing it—*ken me va kerer a mi*, who is going to love me. . . *yo me akodro de akeya noche*, I remember that night....

Now the meat. There it was, a great mass of it on the plate. Her daughter had ground it, it was red and brown and thick and strong, like a man's arm.

She bent more into the big frying pan as she landed the meat in the pot.

"How's it coming, Mom?" her daughter yelled at her, disrupting her concentration. Her daughter was doing a hundred things at once that the mother couldn't contend with.

"Don't hit me," she said under her breath so her daughter wouldn't hear and get mad at her for saying it.

Ah, the meat in the pan, ah there it was courtesy of the silent wooden spoon, the meat snapping and wincing and sliding.

Who was that woman anyway, the mother thought of her daughter, so tall and bossy and busy and sure of herself? I'll just mind my own business. I've got a lot to do, long tasks that require all my concentration so that the matzoh meat will come out beautiful.

"*Bendichas manos!*" she said out loud to herself, with a little cheer. Blessed hands!

The parsley! It was sitting on a table looking forgotten and envious.

Her hands remembered what to do. Take it up in a bunch and put it under the faucet and run the water nice and cool and enjoy the bright happy green of the leaves and stems, such good flavor, such joy, shake it out like a little dance, the green glancing this way and that. Shake out the water! Cut the bunch into small pieces, to her thumb, right over the pot. Ah, the fragrance, her hands were rich with it, *bendichas manos*. It was in with the meat now and she remembered to breathe now that she knew what she wanted to be doing. Had she been stirring with a wooden spoon over flame her whole life, twenty, thirty, forty, fifty years, her whole life, the meat browning, the red thickness pebbling into brown. What was it all about? People were sitting in the other room, but it was none of her business. Her body, her back, her eyes, her hands—she was all there to stir the pot, mash over the pebbled meat, smell the fragrance.

"Sara, what am I doing? I wish I knew," she heard herself say to someone in the kitchen. The answer came back.

"Mom, you're making matzoh meat."

"*Yo me akodro de akeya noche, kuando la luna me enganyo*"—I remember that night when the moon tricked me. Why had she loved that song? It used to make her laugh with pleasure at the angry woman saying what she wanted to say. You should always say what you wanted! When the daughter pushed a bowl of eggs to her, she thought it would be good to crack them and put them in the meat. That came naturally to her.

Each one so perfect in the palm of her hand, then cracked into the plate. No blood! The yolks stared up at her in sheer perfection like the sun, and then slid into the meat. For what?

She knew the wooden spoon would appreciate a chance to go in the meat, that silent tap tap that reminded her of happiness!

And matzoh was right there. White and familiar as if she'd cooked with it all her life, well she had, like manna in the desert. Don't forget that!! She remembered when she was in the desert and the manna came from heaven. You had to soak the matzoh in a dish of broth and then cut it softened into pieces to cover the bottom of the round pan with oil in it hot from the oven. You put the matzoh pieces as a flat bottom to the pan and it came nicely back to her. In went the meat mixture, spread it out, then put a puzzle of matzoh pieces on top, to fit it together as a top layer. Her body bent into the task steadily, her breathing was going right, the way it's supposed to, steady and good, her eye on the ball, just right. Then she straightened up a little, lost in the sunlight of the kitchen, and pulled a chair out away from the kitchen table, to sit down and wait. Her eye fell on some yellow beaten egg in a dish, so she leaned over and took it up and smelled it and then with her fingers feelingly spread it on the top matzoh to give it a juicy shine.

"You did a beautiful job, as always, Mom," said her daughter, and she took the round aluminum pan and slid it into the oven. "Do you want to come in and say hello to everyone?"

"No, I'll sit here and wait."

"But the family is here. In the living room. Everyone wants to hug you and kiss you. Your grandchildren, everyone!"

"*Bueno*," she said but sat resolutely at the table to wait for the *mina*. Really it was enough, and she didn't want to forget what she was doing. She'd rest right there. Out the window, she saw a giddy blue sky that reminded her of all the skies that had spread before her all her life—in the countryside of Turkey, the sky as big as the sea, and she liked the idea of keeping this piece of sky from the kitchen window company after her labors with the matzoh meat.

As she sat, the blue deepened and broadened, deeper, deeper, as if she would swim in it and never know where she was. *Ken me va*, she started humming, *ken me va*, after a pause, *kerer a mi*.

Then "*Bre!* An earthquake!" She yelled so loud everyone came in the kitchen and tried to hug her but she stuck to her chair at the table. "You go ahead," she told them. "I already ate," and she rested her hand on the table to take a nap and slide out of New Jersey, out of the Bronx, out of Brooklyn, out of Harlem, sliding, sliding forward.

The tasty fragrance of the cooked meat and onion and parsley woke her and she stood as if in a dream. There were the potholders and she knew what to do. The blue indigo sky was getting deeper and she heard voices and now was her cue. She took the pan, the *mina de karne* was perfect, she could feel it in her bones, and she took the pan in her protected hands and, her back bent over but her eyes and hands steady, she left the kitchen. There they all were, whoever they were, children and grown-ups, men and women and girls and boys around the table, a whole lot of them as she walked in, the prized pan in front of her, her eyes lowered to her last gift, presented perfectly to the assembled guests of the seder. They were her children and grandchildren, her business partner (her son) from the War, but did she know who they were?

Some months after Passover when her daughter patiently tried to help her shower, she screamed loud, furiously. And she screamed when she went to the door. And she screamed when she went to the top of the stairs. And again the linen closet. It was hard on the patients in the dentist chair downstairs in the daughter's husband's office. So the family all had to confer and come up with a decision, the way they did when one of the granddaughters was eighteen and seeing a married man. We have to solve this together. The Sephardic Home would not take their mother. Finally only a hospital would. It was in Queens. Once there she fell out of bed. They put restraints on her. They tied her to the bed. This was worse than the house in the suburbs, with no one walking around in the street. Nothing here could be understood, only the smell of the walls. This was the end. Her daughter and the sons were grim-faced and horror struck. They all trooped out to Queens to see her. They wept. They smacked their heads. She was gone.

Arlo Guthrie down the hall, visiting his father in the same hospital, came and sang a song in her room after she was gone. He was a boy. He didn't know how dearly beloved she was all those years, or that she always laughed and sang, or that her son was an insurance man, or what insurance was; he didn't know "*Ken Me Va Kerer a Mi*," or the Passover counting song "*Elohenu Shebbah Shamayim*," so he sang what he knew, "This land is my land, this land is your land, from California to the New York island."

Istanbul, Written in the Dark, 1971

THE AMERICAN WOMAN, the retired insurance man's wife, had spent a happy couple of hours with her Turkish cousin and his wife the day before at a café on a wonderfully scenic hill overlooking the Bosphorus, and now she'd come as invited to have dinner at the cousin's apartment. Her cousin and his wife had been detained at the doctor (her own husband would be along later since he was talking to this one and that one about getting his date of birth changed for social security) and so suddenly she found herself alone with her aunt, her mother's sister—(her cousin's mother)—screaming at her.

"They left me here," the woman yelled furiously at her American niece, making her stand totally still as if on alert to avoid blows.

"You, you in America, rich and happy, what do you care that I was left in Turkey, the only one."

The American wife was used to wielding attacks, dishing out her anger like wet knives, but never the other way around. It was a shock, she wouldn't stand for it, this woman had no right—this was shocking.

"My sister, my three brothers, one after the other, America, America, America—they all went, but not me, never me." She was piercing in Ladino, and the American understood every single word, but not a single word. Why was this woman yelling at her, what did it have to do with her, she'd only met her aunt once before, the aunt was living in a distant world, another world.

"And you may think you have nothing to do with this. You're only my sister's daughter. You weren't even born. But that's no excuse. You don't care. Nobody cared. They left me in Turkey like an old rag. Every single one of them left me in Turkey and never looked back. And for what?"

The American wife was outraged to be attacked in this way and her tongue was getting ready to do its own accustomed lashing and respond in kind, the adrenaline charging her blood and her usual fierceness restored to—

"To take care of your grandmother! That's what! Everybody got to leave for America, but I had to stay here to take care of my mother—your grandmother, that's who—your very own grandmother—your mother's mother—and do you think there was anything here—any chance at money, any chance at a husband who could make money—any chance at anything?"

The American woman's self-righteousness rose in a wave, and she began, "How dare you!" but her aunt, cut from the same cloth, but stronger as the genuine Turkish article, cut her off.

"And your mother was the worst, never a letter, never a glance back, never a question of how her poor sister in Turkey is doing, taking care of her old sick mother. NO ONE CARED that I had nothing and was nobody, no one cared."

This was insupportable! the American thought. That she should be attacked for her mother's lack of caring. Did this woman know anything about anything? Yes, they had money and a house in Long Beach but who cares that her sister was left behind sixty years ago—people get left behind and that's their own problem.

"You shut up," she snapped. "You just shut up. I'm not going to take your rage, do you hear me?"

Her aunt went into the kitchen and was banging pots together. The American woman had heard her aunt was a great Sephardic cook, with lemon and onion and spices and parsley, stuffed dolma and tomatoes, stuffed zucchini, but also the arsenic of frustration. No wonder her cousin's wife had an ulcer. They'd lived together all their married life.

And here they were in a pleasant tumult at the door, her Turkish cousin, his wife, and her own husband, overflowing with Ladino warmth and solicitousness and sweetness and they began comparing notes from the day, her husband getting testimonials at the university, her cousin soothing his wife.

The aunt was working away in the kitchen and didn't come out to greet her son and his wife. The stuffed zucchini would be perfect, and the salad, and no one could bear to go into the kitchen to greet her, it was as if they could smell the rage in the well-furnished living room, with its plump chairs and polished tables—the raging woman's son had done well after all, very well, and his gallant courteous manner papered over the difficulties of his mother's fury. He had done very well, magnificently well in import and export, so why didn't she back off, there was nothing to grieve over. She had wonderful smart educated grandsons, the world was open to them—to the children of her children, why not feel pride and charm, relief and pleasure, and she was such a good cook! Why not enjoy what you have, her son never could stop wondering—and an uncle in America had in fact finally helped them with money in those destitute years after his father had gone to Egypt for an operation on his back. But no, she was determined never to get over the rage of violation and injustice. That's what she was broiling with the perfect fish in the kitchen, always broiling, caught in a net of rage, as much as the fish itself, never to get out.

The American woman's husband was continuing the story—it was too exciting, too much fun, too satisfying. It was the social security campaign to prove he was born in 1901. He pulled out a Polaroid picture taken the week before in Canakkale in the Office of the Registrar. The registrar himself, a short man in a cabdriver's cap and summer shirt unbuttoned at the neck, was standing holding open a ledger, as the retired insurance man in a business suit stood beside him holding the edge of the record book.

"What is this?" the cousin asked politely.

"It's proof!" the insurance man said.

"You see," he continued, "they wanted my birth certificate and I didn't have one, so I came back to Turkey to find the proper records."

His wife explained, "Social Security decided he was born in 1905, so he decided as long as they were wrong, he would really correct them, and let them know the truth, that he was actually born in 1901."

"That's why we came to Turkey," he added, "to get this whole thing straightened out."

"You mean you found the page in the book?"

"Can you beat that? There I was listed in that book, just the way I expected."

"Did you take a picture of the page? What did it say?"

"Well, it said I was born in Ottoman Turkish Rumi year 1320, but on the side of the writing there was a note saying my parents corrected it and I was really born in 1318. But where's your mother?" the insurance man interrupted himself.

"She's in the kitchen."

The insurance man went in to find her, to address her with respect and cordiality. He could smell the rage of isolation because she hadn't come out to greet them. He went in the kitchen and took hold of her shoulders that were stiff with apprehension, and as tough as a woman bodybuilder's.

"Ah," he said, "you're the most important one. You are the one person connecting us all. Come in the living room and we'll drink a toast to you, some raki." As he managed to shepherd her in, he kept talking. "You are the one who connects us all, who connects Turkey with the United States, your parents and your children, the very hard times of the past, and the prosperity of the future. You must be so proud of your son—all that he has accomplished is because of your loyalty and devotion—and determination. You took care of your mother, and your father and your son. Everything was terribly hard, but look at what you've accomplished. NO ONE is better than you. NO ONE can hold a candle to you. You are the Jewish heart of Turkey. You are the Jewish heart of the Jewish heart and we love you very much."

With this outpouring she didn't know what to say, except to ignore it all and down her raki and order them all to the big table in the large dining room off to the side.

"A lot of good it does now, it was before when they left me here, I couldn't stand it." She paused as everyone admired her great work, the spread on the table, salads and zucchini stuffed with meat and tomato, okra and rice and beet salad and the fish on a large platter. "I'm not going to forget this unfairness."

The insurance man thought of going behind her chair and placing his good massaging hands on her upper back. This rarely worked with his wife. But he would try. He would press his fingers gently into her upper back, and say sweetly *"we love you, tante,"* and she would relax under his fingertips.

She let him assuage her this way for two minutes but then scraped her chair back as she snapped back to her angry self and left the table to go to her room, and shut the door.

Her son wanted to salvage the dinner as a festive occasion and addressed his guests with warmth and cordiality.

"Tell me more about this social security campaign," he said.

The insurance man was loath to divert from his wife's aunt's claim for justice but at the same time he needed to respect his host's desire to restore the dinner party's dignity. He was torn but the cordial cousin's impulse to restore normalcy to the dinner conversation had precedence over other immediate concerns, so he filled the gap in conversation willingly even though his hosts already knew the particulars he would describe.

The retired man said, "You know of course that Ottoman Turkish Rumi year 1318 must be translated into the date on the Western calendar that Turkey uses now. It coincides with March 15, 1902 to March 14, 1903 in the European calendar.

"Now you'll find it most interesting to know I have always said I was born in February because it is the month of the birthday of the American presidents, George Washington and Abraham Lincoln. I made my date of birth for passports in February for that reason. I did explain that to social security, that we could never know which month we were born in and often picked an exact date according to what we felt at the time, and they were most interested in that fact as I revealed it to them. I added, you see, that when I first applied to the insurance company where I worked for forty-five years, I gave my birthday month as June 1901 because I always saw my arrival in America as the beginning of my life, and I arrived at Ellis Island in June.

"Nonetheless, I subsequently learned from the burial society records that my birth date was in April, and so I will press to be recognized as having been born in the equivalent of April in the year 1318 which would be 1902.

"Of course, I still believe I was born in 1901 as I wrote on my application for the insurance company when I first applied for employment. After all, when I arrived in the U.S. in 1920, the ship manifest said I was eighteen, and in those years families made their children younger to reduce the cost of crossing the ocean, so if I was said to be eighteen, I was probably really nineteen at the time."

His wife's cousin interjected. "You mean you can discuss all of these facts openly with the American government?"

"I must tell you, the American government is the most compassionate and interesting in the world. You can talk everything over and they want to help you."

"This is most unusual," the cousin said.

"They understand the facts of life. You can explain that in Turkey to go into the army in World War I meant you would never be seen alive again. So they understood and respected that a family would want to have certain records that said a remaining son in Turkey was born in 1320 rather than in 1318 or 1317. They never were surprised or questioned the validity of that. For one thing, as it turned out, Turkey was the enemy of the U.S. and, as you know, my two brothers were U.S. citizens and would be fighting against the Turks. Do you think my mother wanted me to face my brothers on a battlefield?"

"You mean to say you could talk openly about these decisions to the American government? I'm most surprised to hear that."

"You know yourself that being Jewish in Turkey was the greatest honor. Nonetheless, you had to be careful. We had a friend of the family who took a walk one day as a child to a little village, and someone noticed him and knew immediately he was a Jew. How, I don't know. I cannot tell you. But the people in the town said, 'Let's kill him, he's a Jew.' This was not the Turkish way, you know that, and indeed a man stepped up, 'oh leave him alone, he's only a boy,' and so they let the boy go. And his son grew up to have an orange drink stand in New York City."

"Orange drink, really?" the cousin said.

"Excellent orange drink. I always used to stop over there to have a nice drink.

"Still, you always had to watch your step. I'm sure it's different now. Look how well you've done. But then it was different, your safety was not assured. And after a millennium of survival through many tragedies, would a Jew really want to subject himself to death in the Turkish army? In any army? A Jew must survive and when the U.S. entered the War in April, 1917, my mother went and said I was born in 1320. She got the court to change the date.

"But now, my dear cousin, let us talk about your mother." He paused. "Although, I'll say one more thing about myself, first. My country knows what immigrants can do. Can you imagine what I gave my country? For forty-five years I worked for the same company, I was a leader, in the first year I sold more than any other agent in the nation, and in my last year when they had to force me to retire— they didn't want me to, of course, I made them so much money for forty-five years that you could fill the ocean with it, I brought them so much business they didn't know what to do for me first, so they let me stay three years more, and then they let me stay an extra month—and the very month I had to retire I was featured in the top business magazine in America. It was a picture of their best salesmen, and there I was, a picture of me.

"And the United States government knew this was because I was an immigrant—full of desire—full of determination—unstoppable, unbeatable—where do you find such inspirational leadership and motivation to make an American company thrive beyond anyone's expectations?"

"Very interesting."

"But your mother, what can we do for her? Does she realize your success and how she helped you and got you through?

"Does she know that you love her and respect her?

"Can you take a trip with her to the U.S.?"

"I know her type," the insurance man's wife piped up. "She'll never get over her anger. Before you arrived, she was yelling at me. She was yelling at me!"

"No, you see," the cousin's wife said, interposing sweetly but realistically. "They decided she should be the caretaking daughter, and when they do that to you they want to keep you down, so you know not to complain, and no matter how you struggle against what is not fair, they keep a pillow on your head, and if you live through it, still you cannot ever really remember how to breathe."

"Her father was very stingy," the cousin said. "Well, then he lost his property and he never knew how to be a poor man with dignity, so he took it out on his daughter—and me. He was nothing and we were even less. I do not like to say these things but they are true."

The insurance man's wife suddenly let out a wail, "Oh, God, the poor woman!" She breathed deeply. "They were torturing her. No wonder she's furious. Women must speak up. I've taught my four daughters that very thing in every word I've ever said. *En boka serada ni entra moshka.* If you keep your mouth shut, not even a fly will get in."

"Well, not to correct you," the insurance man said with a flourish he could not restrain, "but that saying tells you to keep your mouth shut, or else a fly will go in."

"That's the stupidest thing I ever heard. You catch more flies with honey than with vinegar—don't you see of course that no one wants flies, but it's a manner of speaking. *En boka serada*, you can't even get a fly, nothing, zero, so you better speak up, and women here are so tortured I think it's disgusting and a crime.

"On the way to that stinking little town, Canakkale, we saw a blond woman standing just behind a fence staring out at the world. The relative who was taking us around, not that she was a nice woman, she was pretty horrible herself, you should have seen the dump of a hotel she took us to, and she wasn't sorry either, what was she thinking—anyway she said this blond woman's husband kept her locked up in the yard because he was afraid she'd be raped and he'd never be able to keep her after that, they'd both be ruined."

Her husband calmly interjected, still thinking about his host's mother, "Well, what if you and your mother made a trip to New York together, a sort of state visit where all the relatives would invite her to their houses—"

"That's ridiculous," his wife interjected. "She's beyond that."

"I'm afraid your wife is right," the cousin said. "She simply can't get over what happened when she was young and all her sisters and brothers left. That injury she will never get over. We have invited her but she turned it down."

"Her father was too sure he was right," the Turkish wife said. "He needed her to help his dying wife— my mother-in-law was the youngest daughter after all—and therefore once he saw her as that person, he refused to let her see herself any other way; it was for the family and she must sacrifice herself for the family, and everyone knows women sacrifice themselves for the family, and it's what they want, and so they can never depart from that role.

"Especially in Canakkale, they really believed in that. Canakkale was famous for that. They sacrificed themselves willingly and with devotion and love because it was everything for the survival of the family."

"But in this case she didn't want it," the American wife interrupted angrily. "She wanted to get out. She was trapped."

"We must help her," the insurance man said. "What can we do to help her? I know her brothers helped her when she needed money. And even your father came through. But now we must think about how to help her realize what she has accomplished despite very terrible odds. She is like all the Jews; she has persevered despite the most terrible facts to the contrary. How can we help her see the good that she achieved?"

"It's too late," the cousin's wife said quietly. "She has already retaliated making me bear the burden of her rage every day of my life with my beloved husband. I cannot forgive her or begin to help her. I must save myself."

The insurance man's wife looked up surprised at the depth of emotion and the depth of restraint in her cousin's wife's quiet words. The American woman found it very strange to be in Turkey. She'd wanted to travel and feel like the accomplished wife that she was, but she was happier at the Bosphorus café sipping coffee and marveling at the view.

The insurance man had no solution. These people were struggling, and they lived far from New York. He turned to his wife's cousin. "Here I have been praising your mother, but we have said nothing at all about you. Yet, look at what you have accomplished, despite all the forces arranged like a battery of guns to keep you down. You and your wife are the noblest pillars of Istanbul, you and your wife are honorable and forthright, strong and exemplary. I cannot tell you how happy I am to be here today, and to be able to tell you how much you mean to me for your strength and your perseverance. Your sweet generosity and dedication know no bounds, and your children, the finest in the world, will carry forth a banner of well-being to posterity. We are so fortunate to spend this time with you and enjoy your superb hospitality and food."

"His mother cooked the food," the American woman interjected sharply.

"And I will tell you one other thing—that you have honored your mother by living together—keeping the family close is the greatest sign of your worth and value. Despite all your success in business, here is your richest achievement."

He went on. "Can we sing a song to celebrate your honoring each other? Or the prayer that we all know so well?" It was not difficult. They found themselves saying it together, *Ya komimos i bebimos i al dio barukh hu bendeshimos, ke nos dio pan para komer i vidas para vivir kon salu buena*, We ate and drank and we say thanks to blessed God who has given us bread to eat, and our lives to live in good health…."

The insurance wife knew these sentences. For some reason they stood out from the whole morass of Turkish Jewish burdens. So simple, so easy, we ate and drank and we are thankful to be alive.

Saying the words gave her a new idea of how to be happy. "You know," she said addressing her cousin and his wife, "my husband is persevering too. He never lets anything stop him.

"After he was forced to retire, for the previous year he won an award for his salesmanship and the prize was a conference on the West Coast. They were all young men there on their way up. And there he was, already retired! The company had parties for everyone, the wives, the children, we went sightseeing, toured the movie studios. But he sat in the lectures, meanwhile, listening to the VP of the company spur these leaders on to other gains and even higher sales. He took notes on what the speaker said, the big man from the company. 'If you don't do it, nothing will happen. If you don't make the call, you won't serve the community. If you don't make the sale, nothing will move forward. Service is our motto, and service is our inspiration.'"

"Yes," said her husband, "that's exactly what I mean. Look at your cousin here, who has figured out exactly what to do, although his mother was angry and bitter, his father was dead, and his grandfather was holding back from supporting him. He persevered and his grandfather came through with the help he needed."

"I just thought it was funny that on your retirement as you scribbled these notes in the convention bulletin, your final note was to explain why your handwriting wasn't the best. You wrote and underlined how you took these notes—you jotted down that these inspirational thoughts which excited you from the company vice president were 'written in the dark.'"

"You're right," he said. "You saw that. That was true, and true it is that I love my beautiful wife and my four beautiful daughters."

"And he loves the U.S. and he will love social security when they compromise with him on his date of birth. He won't get the 1901 he wanted, but I can tell you no one is a match for his perseverance and determination. My guess, it will take another year or two for him to be sure of it, but finally they'll call it a draw, and give him 1903," she said, and then, "I think we should help you clear the table from this wonderful meal and then we'll go back to our hotel."

"One other thing," her husband added. "Tomorrow at the hotel we'll send a bouquet of flowers to your mother. She's a heroine and we want her to know we love her."

The Atlantic Ocean, 2008

The Atlantic Ocean in Long Beach was calm, and so was the insurance man's widow on her noodle. It was morning and serene, as new as a child's first day of summer, and she could not have been more thrilled to be in the ocean, a granddaughter on her left, a grandson on her right. The two of them were talking but doing their job of protecting her from drowning, and she didn't have to listen to a word they said. They boldly faced outward, the lap of the ocean, the three of them. She liked that.

Now ninety-seven, in her last few years, she had finally learned the art of happiness. It had been her husband's way, and she had hated him for it all their lives. Everyone else loved him for it, and that was galling. He was always generous, eager to please, with sunny good will and good humor; he was willing to go the extra mile for anyone, and that brought him irredeemable pleasure in a way that made others happy too, not just himself. His anxiety, of course, never left him. Well, that flaw had given her an opening to make him suffer, and she had risen to the challenge of that pleasure as often as she wanted.

But now she tried his way. How easy it was to let all that fall away, now that the house was gone and all the papers and bills, all the small cheap paper plates she wrote phone numbers on and dates when the children called.

Something about Uganda drifted from the girl between gulls' cries. She, the widow, had done that. She thought, I'm still here. "We went on a safari there" might have come out some earlier day, but not today. The ocean took away her need for words.

"Cell phones?" her grandson said to his cousin.

Cell phones! a gull cried, then flew high overhead with a clam in its beak—heading to the jetty to smash it there for the breakfast special.

The noodle was stiff pastel green foam and, bowed over in its hard starchiness, made a gentle arc between the widow's legs. Her joy was as big as the salt water, that rippling lake all around her. "I'm still here," she sang out to herself.

"You know I spent a year with the coffee farmers," the granddaughter said.

"You don't even drink coffee," her cousin ribbed her.

"You remembered that! You're good!

"Coffee is the great hope of the country. And farming. We know these farmers are heroic, working the land. And the U.S. dumping on the markets, even well-intentioned with aid, destroyed production."

The ocean rolled them gently, lovingly, and they were both holding onto their beloved grandmother in the simplest most affirmative way, so she hardly felt it yet she felt safe like the child of a good mother.

Was it all right to let her stay in the water so long, they worried. It was twenty minutes already.

"I feel young," the ninety-seven-year-old burst out as if she heard their concerns, but she hadn't of course. Young people stayed and stayed in the ocean this way, sitting on a noodle. She was still there and young!

They'd picked her up from the assisted living, who knew what was right?

"The farmers had a problem," the granddaughter said. "I'll give you the short version. They needed to know stuff, about soil, weather, pests, pesticides. What they needed was computers so they could get important information to make a success of farming. But there was no infrastructure for computers, nothing, so it was looking bleak."

"Can you hold her a minute while I swim a little?"—

"Go, it's fine." He dived and played and gamboled in the perfect day, body-surfed two miniscule waves, then came right back.

"So one of the farmers told me he had an idea. He was young, tall, muscular and said they urgently need to get this information somehow," she went on.

The grandma was still lilting in the ocean, all the years behind her letting her remember who she was, she nagging and nudging to get the whole family into the water, aren't you going in, no jellyfish, no seaweed, no broken shells underfoot, and as soon as someone went in, her hand was waving wildly, "you're out too far…"

Angry, anxious, insistent, jealous, that's what she'd been, that they dared enjoy themselves so lusciously, yet they were her children, and their spouses, in the ocean, dawdling and diving, careening, daring, ignoring her angry calls.

"The young man took me aside one day and said he had the answer. He looked at me and said, with triumph shining in his eyes: cell phones. He was right, brilliant. The farmers can call in, whenever they need, to a Kampala call center and ask a question, get an update, a consultation. They do it! It works! They find out what they need to know. They have someone to consult with."

She broke away now to bodysurf two ridiculously small waves.

Then Grandma was ready to leave the water. Suddenly she was ready.

"I've had enough! Help me go back to the chair," she shouted, as if they were hard of hearing. So they did.

"We got a grant, we wrote the proposal together. The grant paid for it all, the staffed research lab, the call center, the cell phones for hundreds of farmers. It's all in place, so I came home for a visit."

Her cousin helped his grandmother out of the water.

"Here I am!" the granddaughter said, her arms spread wide.

GLOSSARY

ALLIANCE ISRAELITE UNIVERSELLE: As the Ottoman Empire spiraled downward, the plight of its impoverished Jews came to the attention of wealthy educated French Jews who in 1860 established this extensive system of schools. Its Paris-trained teachers brought French to cities big and small throughout the Levant, giving Ottoman Jews a glimpse of the Western world.

TALMUD TORAH: Talmud Torah refers to the study of Torah and a school or a system of schools that start children with a religious education, important because religious learning is to take place from the cradle to the grave. In late Ottoman Turkey, these schools were under-funded and old-fashioned.

TORAH: The first five books of the Hebrew Bible, known as the Five Books of Moses, make up the Torah, the core text of Judaism. Synagogues have the Torah hand-written on a great scroll wrapped in a velvet cloak: the two wooden handles of the scroll point upward and are topped in many synagogues with sterling silver or other ornamental bells. For the weekly readings of the Torah, the cloak and bells are removed before and replaced afterwards.

SIMCHAT TORAH: This fall holiday celebrates the completion of the week-by-week communal reading of the Torah over the course of the year; a procession of congregants makes seven circuits of the synagogue holding all the synagogue's Torah scrolls, singing as they go, and sometimes continuing the celebration outdoors.

SHALACH MANOT: the pen name of the author. In Hebrew, *shalach manot* refers to the gifts of food Jews give to friends and relatives on the holiday of Purim.

TURKISH JEWS: In 1492, when the Jews were expelled from Spain where they had lived for a thousand years and achieved great success in the sciences, arts, medicine and other fields, the Sultan of the Ottoman Empire welcomed the exiles to populate his large empire newly acquired in 1453. Keeping their Jewish beliefs, prayers, rituals, and communal cohesion, the Turkish Jews also maintained the Spanish language as their mother tongue, writing it in Hebrew characters—as well as many Spanish customs, cooking traditions, and songs. The Jews of Turkey, like the Ottoman Empire itself, went through periods of prosperity and decline. Jews were a smaller minority than either the Armenians or the Greeks, and enjoyed the protection of the state and the opportunity to rule their own communities because of their belief, like that in Islam, in one God. Also, for the most part, they were not subject to pogroms or persecutions, and had the benefits of benign neglect. However, they were viewed as inferior to the Muslims, and developed a diplomatic carefulness that allowed them to maintain their dignity without ever offending their Turkish hosts. Today about 17, 000 Jews live in Turkey.

TURKISH REFORMS OF 1908: The Young Turks in 1908 established an egalitarianism that sounds attractive to our contemporary American ears, but to the Jews of that era, it meant they were now citizens and thus subject to conscription into the Turkish army, a dire and frightening reality Jews tried to avoid at all costs. This change and the economic deterioration of the empire spurred a Jewish wave of emigration.

THE U.S. IMMIGRATION ACT OF 1924: A follow-up to the 1921 Act, the Immigration Act of 1924 further limited immigration to the United States, virtually closing the door for non-"Nordic" immigrants. That door would not open again until 1965 when, with the Cold War, the United States decided to trump the Russians by opening the nation to immigration by many peoples, including blacks of many nationalities, who had long been kept out.

ACKNOWLEDGMENTS

WHY A PEN NAME? When I began to write Sephardic fiction in 2002, I saw my writing as a way to honor gifts passed down to me, stories and songs that embody a way of seeing the world. We're Turkish Jews on both sides of my family. In our history, life was good, beautiful even, as well as harsh, and prayer was an expression of a state of being, of gratitude. Shalach Manot as a phrase captures that feeling. It refers to gifts of food for friends and family on Purim.

I'm grateful to Rabbi Marc D. Angel, a bold Jewish leader and award-winning writer who has illuminated Sephardic Judaism and been a great teacher in his over thirty books. Rabbi Angel has asked me to write for his journal, *Conversations*, and introduced me to Netanel Miles-Yépez, the publisher of Albion-Andalus Books.

I'm fortunate to have as a brilliant and caring friend Angela Wigan, co-author of our book, *A Short and Remarkable History of New York City*. In recent years, she and I went on to meet regularly on a bench by the Hudson River, bikers daringly speeding by as we each were immersed in writing our own novels.

Others also read the manuscript or excerpts and gave invaluable feedback or provided help in other ways: Leo Haber, Rickie Solinger, Shira Dicker, Jesse Epstein, Elisabeth Gitter, Ellen Geiger, Deborah Manion, Carole Harris, Ursula Bentele, Lory Hammack, Lewis Bateman, Brenda Rodrigues Epstein, George Blecher, Toni Levi, Gerald Sorin, Nina Bannett, Joyce Morgenroth, Regina Mushabac, and Phyllis Kantar.

A Mellon Fellowship allowed me time to write this book and introduced me to remarkable artists like Kelly Anderson and Reiner Leist. Three creative writing grants from the City University of New York (CUNY), through its Professional Staff Congress and Research Foundation, were also crucial in giving me time to write, as was a fellowship leave provided by the CUNY campus where I teach, City Tech. An award for my manuscript from the Leapfrog Press international fiction contest meant a great deal. My City Tech colleagues and students have been inspiring.

How can I begin to thank my parents, Estelle Mushabac and Victor Mushabac? They were dynamos in their love of life, their love for each other and for their children and grandchildren.

Above all I thank my husband, Arthur Morgenroth, whose humor and generosity are bigger than any acknowledgment can say. He is a thinker, a storyteller—it's an immense gift to be in a lifelong conversation with him. I also thank our sons, David, Daniel, and Benjamin Morgenroth, and our daughters-in-law, Loriana Berman and Rebecca DeCola, for their great inventive spirit and warmth.

Shalach Manot is the pen name of a writer who lives in a New York City apartment looking out on a brick wall. Manot's credits include fellowships from the Mellon Foundation and City University of New York; short stories, essays, and an NPR play about the Spanish Jews; and the award-winning *A Short and Remarkable History of New York City.*